The Townsman

Thomas F. Sheehan

Pocol Press

Punxsutawney, PA

POCOL PRESS
Published in the United States of America
by Pocol Press
320 Sutton Street
Punxsutawney, PA 15767
www.pocolpress.com

Publisher's Cataloguing-in-Publication

Names: Sheehan, Thomas F., 1928-, author.
Title: The townsman / Thomas F. Sheehan.
Description: Punxsutawney, PA, Pocol Press, 2022.
Identifiers: LCCN: 2021952432 | ISBN: 979-8-9852820-0-9
Subjects: LCSH Cowboys--Fiction. | Indians of North America--
Fiction. | Frontier and pioneer life--West (U.S.)--Fiction. | West
(U.S.)--History--Fiction. | Western stories. | Short stories. |
BISAC FICTION / Westerns | FICTION / Historical / General
Classification: LCC PS3569.H39216 T69 2022 | DDC 813.6--
dc23

Library of Congress Control Number: 2021952432

ACKNOWLEDGEMENTS

Stories in this collection, over a stretch of time, have appeared in various sites or presentations on-line such as *Facebook*, *Rope and Wire Western-Style Magazine*, *Frontier Tales*, *Literally Stories*, *Merida Review*, *Danse Macabre*, and *Cowboy Jamboree*. Some stories were presented in sites or magazines that are now defunct. All rights belong to me, Tom Sheehan, as author and agreement.

TABLE OF CONTENTS

Weber's General Store   1
The Last Train to Silver Creek   7
The Freighter's Return Engagement   13
The 2nd Dead Horse Saloon   19
The Bridgetown Bard   25
The Dam at Wasahoa   31
Jehrico's Wolf Pup   36
The Barber's Romance   42
Texas Town   47
The Black   54
The Circus in the Valley of Ten Chiefs   60
The Raggedies   69
Coachman's Find   82
Secret of the Cave   92
Doc Hannah Goes to Town   100
Shooter in Buckskin   105
Doc Hannah's Honeymoon   111
Doc Hannah's Replacement   115
The Barber of Copa Verdi   122
Exodus Two, Western Style   129

"Go out and help unload that wagon, Nate," Lucas Weber said, "and be careful of the peaches. Make sure you put them all in the right place." Weber owned the general store in San Remo, the biggest store in the territory, and he kept two freighters busy all the time, and he knew cans of peaches were a great delicacy for drovers and chuck wagon cooks; but that wasn't all that he had in his message. His helper at odd times was Nate Witham, the son of a neighbor. As Weber spoke, he kept eyeing the strange customer in the corner of the store, a man he had never seen before in the store, or in San Remo for that matter, and saw the man reach slowly down inside his heavy coat. Weber knew he was drawing a weapon. Weber's order to young Witham heading out the door carried one more element, "And make sure the wagon ammo box is full." He waved the youngster out of the store.

Young Witham, barely 13 by a few days, was out the door and going around the corner, even as the stranger turned to face Weber, a pistol in his hand. "No noise, mister. All I want's the money in the cash box and you won't get kilt."

"I understand, mister," Weber said. "I've been robbed before and I know just what to do." His hands were in the air when the robber said, "Put them hands down. You don't have to do that to let people know you're being robbed, in case they look in when they go past." He looked over his shoulder to see if any other customers were on the way in or going by.

Waving the pistol at Weber, he said, "I ain't goin' to hurt you, mister. I just got hungry kids and I can't do much anymore, so don't do anythin' funny."

"I have kids of my own," Weber said, "four of them, none of them old enough to work here yet, but they're coming along soon enough to do a job. How many kids do you have?"

"I've got four too, but none of them's got a job to step into when the time comes. I ain't even got that." The look on his face said he was getting nervous.

Weber thought the man looked hungry as well as undernourished. He thought about the load of canned peaches due soon and not yet outside, as he had told Lucas.

"Is this your first robbery?" Weber said, deciding to take a chance.

"How'd you know that?" The robber's face was lit up by surprise.

1

"You want a job?" Weber said. "You can help me. You better put up that gun before the sheriff gets here and locks you up for good."

"How's he gonna do that? He don't even know I'm here with this gun on you."

"He knows now, mister. The boy that ran out went right to him and told him I was going to get robbed. He'll be here in a few minutes. Better put that gun away. We'll tell him it was a joke."

"How's he know?"

"Remember the last thing I told the boy?"

"Yuh, you said make sure the wagon ammo box is full."

"Exactly. That's my warning message that there's trouble here. Only used it one other time. The robber got killed by the sheriff on his way out the door."

This robber, caught up in a whole lot of self-argument and measurement, put the gun in his waist band, just before the sheriff came rushing in the door.

Sheriff Bob Talcott, gun in hand, said to Weber, "What's going on here, Lucas? You got trouble?"

"No, Bob, I just hired me a new store man and we practiced our alert signal on Nate. It worked pretty good, didn't it? He got down there to warn you in a hurry, I was showing the new gent who'll be working for me."

The sheriff put out his hand. "Glad to meet you, mister. You got a good boss there, and sharp as they come. I guess you seen that already. I didn't get your name."

"My names Lennie Caprio. I'm from down Rutledge way and movin' my family up here. They be here next week."

"You looking for a place for them?"

"I reckon I'll be doin' that, soon's they get here."

"Well, if Lucas here's hiring you, my old place is up for rent, real cheap as it needs a whole wagonload of work. But it does have a roof on it. You handy at all?"

"I can do a few things ordinary like."

"Good enough for me," the sheriff said and put out his hand again. "Come by when you can talk about things. Lucas'll tell you where I'm at if you can't find me." He laughed and left, picking up a penny candy as he left, saying, "This one's on the house, right, Lucas, for my quick response time?" He laughed again.

The bonhomie touched at Caprio as real.

2

The next day Weber introduced him to the trade, but the two talked a great deal during the day, during slow moments or tedious duties that demanded friendly chatting.

Caprio told him about himself, letting go some things he had held inside for a long stretch, like almost his whole life. "My parents brought me from Italy when I wasn't a year old, more or less. I don't remember none of it or the first few years, but we were coming out here and they both got killed in a raid. Not Indians, but white renegades. And they took everything in our wagon, but I was hid out by my father. I must have been the only one left because a posse came and one fellow took me to their town. I bounced around forever until I got work here and there, doing everything I could, but I never met a man as good as you on the quick. I mean that. My family will love you, knowing we got a chance. I had a ranch stole right out from under me because I was from Italy. They plain didn't like me or my kind and plain stole it and told me they'd kill my wife and kids if I did anything stupid. I didn't move a muscle because they were all I had in the whole damned world."

Weber was irate at what happened. "Sounds like a real bunch of range rats, that crew. Didn't anyone help you? The law? Nobody?"

"The law was in on it I heard later. All the way. I was a hundred miles away and spreading it more when I heard how real crooked the whole deal was. My wife didn't dare go back, not with four kids. And I couldn't make her."

"That sheriff still on the job down there?" Weber stared into Caprio's dark eyes.

"No, he don't do any more sheriffing. Makes more money working on the other side. But one day he'll get evened with. That's for sure."

"Caprio," Weber told the sheriff a few weeks later, "is a good worker. Learns real fast. I bet he's a better grocer man than he is a cow man. Has he done any work on your place?"

"Damned if he hasn't Lucas. He got some of the roof repaired I didn't even see as bad, and has the whole place caulked and mudded up, like it's tight now for cold weather coming. Place looks real homey and his wife is good at house doing, real good. We lucked out, you and me."

"And him," Weber said. "He lucked out too. But there's something else with him, Bob. He's got an eye for things, I swear."

3

The sheriff had a wide smile on his face as he said, "Like what? You ain't getting holy on me, are you, Lucas? What're you talking about?"

"One thing leaps up at me. He has a flair for attracting the women in town."

"You saying he's a romancer?"

"No, not that way, Bob, and I'm not getting holy on you either. He brings women in because he knows how to dress up my displays. He's like a magician with them. They buzz around clothes and dresses and bonnets like they're bees at the hive. It's like a new part of the store, but he says his wife gives him ideas."

"Well, he's no god then. What else he got cooking in you?"

"He says things that come around, just like he said they would. Told me to cut back on my peach orders and get more pears. Says it's in the weather. Damned if I didn't sell every can of pears I got and only half the peaches from last time, and people still asking for pears, like they got the real hungers."

"So, you can't make a judgment on that. Could be good guessing, coincidence, more luck on his part like he's on a streak. He doesn't play cards, does he?" The laugh was there again for the sheriff and a slap on the back of the grocer.

"It's not like that, Bob," Weber said. "He doesn't bring things up so he can talk about them. It always happens when I say something and whatever it is comes to him. He's not bashful telling me what he feels. I know he's not afraid of being wrong, but he just isn't, not any of the time. It's kind of eerie if you ask me."

The sheriff said, "You got him all practiced up on the alarm system you got going?" His hearty laugh was an aside comment.

"Oh, hell, Bob he's practiced that to perfection. Knows everything I ever told him." The grocer paused, thought about the conversation and said, "That's enough of that, Bob. How's it going with you? The town seems quiet now, quiet as I've ever seen it. It's been pleasant, that's for sure."

"Strange you say that, Lucas. I've been getting the feeling that I'm missing something I should be seeing, like a turn's being made, a change or something coming on the wind, and I can only feel it but see nothing of it. At least, not yet."

Now it was the storekeeper's turn to laugh. "You say that after what we talked about on Caprio. How do you feel now, wearing my boots?"

4

"Yuh, I know. Odd as hell. Can't put my finger on it, so keep your eyes open all the time." The sheriff, in a quick turn, walked out of the store without taking his usual piece of penny candy.

Weber took note of the omission.

One afternoon a week later, Weber looked up as his wife was closing a sale with a stocky man he had not seen before. The man had a new Colt in his hands and checked it out three or four times, feeling the balance in the weight, the movement of the trigger, the comfort zone in his hand. He was standing at the weapons counter after checking out several other guns.

"It appears to be just what I'm looking for, Ma'am," the man said, his voice deep and resonant and carrying itself out to the stockroom where Caprio came to attention. He listened to the words, not really hearing them, but only the tone in them, the recognition in them.

At first he was stupefied, believing he knew who the speaker was.

"I'll take it, Ma'am, and two boxes of ammunition," the customer said, closing out the sale, "and one of them there Stetsons, the light gray one being the one I like best. You wrap them up in a bag for me and I'll be back to pick them up and settle the bill. I'm going down to the saloon for a drink. It's been a long ride today for me and my boys and I'm partial to wetting my throat in this situation."

Caprio yelled from the back of the store, "Hey, boss, I got to make sure the ammunition box is full on the wagon. I'll be right back."

Weber was at attention behind the counter, while his wife, whom he had not let in on any alarm signals, wanting her out of the way by any means he could use, said to the customer, "You go right ahead and have your drink. I'll have them ready when you come back, or my husband will. He'll be here until closing time, around 9 o'clock, because it's a Saturday." She smiled as the customer left the store.

"Land's sakes, Lucas, what was Lennie talking about? What ammo box?"

"Oh, it's nothing, dear, but you can go now. Lennie and I will take care of things. And Bob'll be coming in soon, too."

She kissed him on the cheek and said, "You're the boss," and added, "here anyway." She too had a parting laugh as she went out the rear door.

5

Caprio and the sheriff came in a few minutes later, with the sheriff leading the way and asking Weber right away what was going on. "You gents'll have me spinning in place?"

"Lennie's got this one, Bob. Let him tell you."

Caprio told him the whole story, the one he told Weber about losing his small ranch. "That man here was the old sheriff down there near Rutledge. He said he has his men here. I don't think they're goin' to rob the store, but I bet they'll try the bank."

"You sure on this, Lennie?" both men said in unison. Their earlier subject of conversation was out in the open. Now, action was required.

Weber said, "You feel pretty sure it's the bank they want?"

Caprio, looking both men in the eyes in turn, said, "Not enough here for them. With a good cash drawer there at the saloon, that's the only other place, but there's too many people around the saloon."

"By God, I think he's right," Talcott said. "I'll get the deputies and appoint a few more."

He looked at Caprio, the new hire with the voice of wisdom, and knew he could count on him. "Lennie, you slip out to the barber shop. That friendly Saturday night poker game is being played right now in the back room. Tell those boys I need them here, come in the back way. Tell them to bring their weapons. There'll be six or seven of them there and we can use them all."

His voice had already risen a few octaves, and his eyes had further lit up, for action was at hand and the sheriff was about to go to work. It was all part of the divine plan of good and bad, meek and powerful, the haves and the have nots, and generally came to confrontation before resolution.

The story still makes the rounds, down near San Remo and Rutledge and all the stops in between, how one bank robbery, engineered by a crooked and former sheriff, was halted, without a single shot being fired by either side, by the intervention of a clerk at Weber's General Store. The gang was caught coming out of the San Remo Bank, bags of money in their hands, stuffed in their pockets, under their hats, only to face the sheriff, a handful of deputies, a small army of citizens, and the new clerk at the general store nodding with a new-found retribution and revenge for past sins committed by the crooked sheriff.

6

The Last Train to Silver Creek

At Silver Creek, on a lengthy local branch of the Wyoming-Idaho-Montana Pacific Railroad, which too many people for too long had called the Wimpy Line, the last train ever to come to Silver Creek, in the Territory, and the local mine operation, gave off its whistle and started the transfer of steam power to its wheels. A Cloud of black smoke rose from the engine and climbed into the morning air. Not a soul stood on the station platform to witness the last train to be sent there, a train whose engine was preceded on the tracks by two flat cars loaded with dynamite, packed to the hilt with dynamite bound to explode on impact, as designed.

The plan, devised by mine owners and their engineer, was to destroy any access to the mine so nobody could get inside "ever again," where two collapses in a week had claimed the lives of 17 men. To be honest, the mine had petered out earlier and was not worth any further investment, and the deaths of 17 men had infuriated the small town and all its neighbors. Every nickel's worth of silver had long been found and extracted. It appeared to all interested parties that the last futile efforts searching for silver were the hopes of a few hungry men looking for one more pay-off.

The mine engineer had ordered a spur track on an existing slight downward grade to be laid right into the entrance of the mine, as deep as they could go in the old "as wide as two oxen in traces" concept upon which railroad widths were constructed in narrow spaces. The two blast cars would roll downhill, once freed of the connection to the engine, until the second was set off and the first car would then expand the thrust, and the damage, deeper within the mine.

He kept talking about the responsibility, and dangers, of setting off a simple pile of dynamite at the entrance or just inside; he didn't want any part of more deaths if something happened during such an exercise. A cache of dynamite near the entrance might allow entrance later on; a cache deeper in the mine might lead to another cave-in. So, with all that in mind, he developed the plan to use two old flat cars, practically from the rust pile, to support the effort. Talk kept coming from him about setting off the second car first so the first car, further into the mine, would then set off a deeper explosion, with attendant thrust to insure the collapse of the mine's interior.

7

The engineer's voice kept advising, and hoping, "And never again can this mine cause deaths," so with that admonition he left town once his plan was accepted and deployment staged.

But things went wrong right from the start.

It was evident with the mine gone that the town would die a slow death, fade at its roots. Everything in Silver Creek, of token or substance, was moving. Many people had already left. The signs could be read easily if one looked about: few people were in the main street, shop doors were closed or boarded up, signs taken down, and the livery, usual hub of a town's activity, was empty. Those who were still in town were packing up their property, preparing to leave.

Silver Creek's outgoing sheriff, Colin Grafton, who had been summoned to Spottsville in two weeks to discuss a new assignment, sat on his mount on the start of the downward grade when the two cars were cut loose from the engine. Inertia, never to be messed with, sat dumb and inactive on the tracks as the two flat cars did not move. The train engineer and the fireman gave an inept push, turned around and looked back at the one official who had stayed behind, a clerk, who shook his head and walked away, already on his own way out of Silver Creek, severing all ties.

From off the side of the newly-laid track, a spur into Hell as one man had called it, came a tall and gangly man with his horse and a rope. He tied the rope to the front of the first car and urged his horse to "Lay it on, Bessie! Lay it on!"

The horse, a good-sized animal, strained, caught an edge of inertia, and the cars started down the grade. The man gave the two-car unit time to get going. When the gangly man tried to untie the rope, the horse stumbled, he fell from the saddle, and the horse, regaining its stride, ran alongside the two cars picking up speed. The man screamed that his leg was hurt and he couldn't get to his horse to release her.

Grafton, back up the spur, saw the rope coming taut between the horse and the lead car as the cars, though lumbering along, picked up more speed. Grafton loved his own mount, Catdance, a six-year friendship between the two. The understandable cries of Bessie's owner came to him and he wondered what kind of a knot the man had tied on his horse's pommel. The cars continued to increase their speed and the horse, now caught up taut by the rope, and ran alongside the lead car, dangerously close to getting pulled under the wheels.

Grafton suddenly spurred his horse and took off down the short length of track. The clerk, well behind Grafton, and well out of dynamite blast range, screamed at him: "Look out, Sheriff. It's going to blow up when it hits."

The sheriff didn't hear him yelling and kept racing after Bessie, now alarmed by the strange force pulling her. Grafton knew there was not much time. He pulled his pistol and started shooting at the taut rope. He did not hit it until his third shot, the tension finally making the break in the rope.

But the freed horse continued down the tracks. Grafton made one more rush, caught up with the animal, grabbed the reins, turned her around, and headed back up the spur.

The blast behind him was a horrendous sound and he feared he would die from fragments thrown through the air with enormous force, or Catdance would get killed or Bessie. Low in the saddle he went, the way he'd seen Indians ride on raids, when a piece of rock flew past his head with a rushing sound in its wake. It was a frightening sound, a frightening thought, and he kept as low as he could. A glancing blow on his shoulder told him some piece of rock or other debris had hit him, and he felt lucky it had not been slammed at his head.

Shards and pieces of debris of all kinds moved through the air with whistles and moans attached, a frightening mixture of danger and noise eternity riding between each pellet-like missile. He imagined pieces of steel or iron from the flat cars were now part of the flying mixture. Noise was power and power was speed was a rush of air. The mountain shook and he swore the whole ridge beyond him moved in the burst. Catdance, aware of some odd circumstance taking place, went faster, even as the air became filled with more pellets of various sizes. Bessie, by fortune, kept pace, already having run one race for life.

The clerk, taking a deep breath of relief as he saw Grafton and the two horses get back to the top of the incline, suddenly spun round as a huge piece of the mountain off to his left blew open and dust and noise and debris were blasted out through a new opening in the mountain, as if making up for the shutting down of the main entrance. He quickly understood the enormous pressure that had been created inside the mine and how it had gone looking for release, for the weakest deterrent to movement, and found it in the side of the mountain.

Debris from the new hole in the mountain rained down on the train engine as it sat still on the tracks. A sudden spurt of steam

9

revealed a break of some sort in the steam line or the boiler, and the engineer and the fireman ran away from the engine as volatile live steam started to pour with a great rush from an undetermined part of the engine.

Grafton got the gangly man to get up on Bessie and the two riders went away from the mountain and the debris in the air and the threat of the steaming engine. He wondered, immediately, if the engine would be abandoned in its place. Would it be worth a massive salvage effort out here in a town soon to be dust, beside a mine that had gone dead flat in its yield? He had no answers, but could not envision the owners spending more money.

The gangly man said, "You saved both me and Bessie, Sheriff. I can't say enough for that, 'cept I'm breathin' and I guess you are too." He pointed at the clerk, now on his horse, riding away from the collapsed mine, the town soon dead, and an engine running out of steam. "Don't that all look like the damned end of the world, Sheriff? Him ridin' off like that?"

Grafton said, "That's the last train in here and the last mine man out of here. Sure does look like the end. Where are you headed, and what's your name? I know your horse's name is Bessie. I saw you come in on the train about a week ago and haven't seen you since."

"Oh, I'm not leavin', Sheriff. I'm stayin'. I bought the mine from the owners 'cause they bought it from my father. He made 'em write up in the agreement that they had to sell it back to him or to me if they was ever goin' to sell it. And my name is Spruce Therrien and my father was Alfonse Therrien and he found the first bit of silver here and opened up his claim and mined it for a couple of years, small stuff, until they bought it from him, the way I said. He always told people, and those who wanted to buy it, that he didn't think they'd be enough silver for more than a family, but they believed he had hit a big one. They got enough to make a few of them rich, but they ran out when it ran out. I own it now. You interested in bein' partners with me? No man I'd rather share it with than you."

"Oh, I'd have to give that a heap of thinkin'," Grafton said, "'cause I'm no minin' man and I guess I got a new job waitin' on me if I want it."

"You don't have to be no minin' man, Sheriff. I know it all. My pa taught me the whole rope, and then some. 'Don't ever let go what you own like I did,' he said. So that caution is mine now. I just need company for a while 'cause it looks like the

10

whole shootin' match is leavin' town, but somethin' my pa said about this mine not yet bein' itself has stuck in my craw since the day he died."

Grafton, thinking about the old days when words and promises ran true to form, kept hearing the words of the elder Therrien. And he found himself putting a lot of faith in them. "Maybe I'll dance on your ticket for a while, Spruce. Can't hurt me none if I don't have to go down inside that almighty fearsome thing." He pointed at the mine, and the smoke still sitting above the one-time entrance like a black cloud in a bad sky.

The pair caught up with the mining clerk, who turned to them and said to Therrien, "I hope things can be pleasant for you and you find a little bit of silver here and there, but don't get your dreams in a big lather. The big boys don't exactly walk away from a two dollar bill if they can help it. They just figure it's not worth their fight to keep going. Even had a hard time among themselves springing for the cost of the dynamite."

Everything must have shot through his mind and he finally said, "I'm glad I'm shuck of the place, as they say out this way. I'm heading back to Illinois and the big city. I'm going to open up a men's shop. Always wanted that. Sure did."

He spurred his horse and said, "The agreement is nice and clean, so don't worry about anything. Good luck." He was on the dead run in seconds.

Therrien, looking all over the terrain, seeing the state things were in, kept nodding his head. "I think my pa was right on this thing. I'm goin' to give it my best shot. I'd sure like to have you with me, Sheriff. I'm the kind of guy who likes company, and you're about the best company that's come along for me in a long while. Sure is." He patted the neck of his horse, and said, "Ain't that right, Bessie? Ain't I plumb right about all that?"

The two potential new partners in an old holding sat on top of a higher grade and kept looking at the scene in front of them.

Grafton, musing to himself, finally said, "Up in Spottsville they have a mine too. Keeps the place going like this mine did for Silver Creek. But who says it won't go the same way and fold in on itself like this one did and then dry up the whole town. I'm not one for repeating mistakes. Maybe I will take a run at it with you." He put out his hand to shake Therrien's hand and said, "Does this make it a deal as good as the written one you got from the mine owners?"

11

"It sure does, Sheriff. Now I'd like to call you by your name proper, 'cause I don't figure you to be sheriff here much longer than today by the look of those wagons marchin' out of here amid all this ruckus."

He pointed to a line of wagons slowly on the move, putting distance between them and Silver Creek and the dead mine.

Grafton said, "My name's Colin and you're Spruce and that's how we'll handle it from here on."

They shook hands again, and Therrien said, almost as an aside, "Bein' the minin' man in this here new partnership, I'm goin' over there where that mountain got busted loose and take a look at what kind of innards it has that were tossed out at that end."

Bessie stepped off and entered ground that a bit earlier had been deluged with a torrent of debris from the new hole in an old mountain. Therrien guided his horse gingerly through the mass of debris, alighted from the saddle, picked up the first hunk of rock he touched, studied it, and looked over his shoulder directly at Grafton. His voice rose with a certain ring to it, a certain clarity, but there was only one listener.

Therrien, with an added sense of pride in his voice, yelled loudly, "My pa was not wrong for a minute about this claim, Colin. Look what we got here," and he held up the object in his hand, waved it in the air, and yelled again, "Gold. Gold as pure as I ever saw it."

The new partnership in Silver Creek, as could be seen, was on solid ground, while the engineer was gone, the clerk out of sight, and the previous owners already down the trail a long stretch.

Silver Creek, as the story goes, just had to have a new name.

The Freighters' Return Engagement

Earl Friscoe and Buckeye Davidson were freighters for a long time and had weathered a few storms along the way, but the one they endured on the Shiloh Two road from Friscoe's hometown of Mesa Cappo was the only one they went back to and spent time on; all the other losses were written off as part of the big gamble from the beginning.

There was something different about this one.

On this particular trip the partners were hauling cans of peaches and cans of pears for the Shiloh Two General Store, among other things, and a few wooden barrels of whiskey for Miles Redding at the Lost Mine Saloon, Shiloh Two's finest. The cans of fruit, favorites of cowpunchers on the trail and, of course, the chuck wagon cooks, were picked up at a rail stop, delivered there from Louisiana and other good-growth land that lived on water from the Mississippi River and moisture from the Gulf of Mexico. The whiskey, as with all earlier pick-ups, had come from an Old Crow House distillery at Carson Wells. Bourbon or rye, whatever it was brought out as, came in rugged barrels made of white oak, declared best for the product for man's best taste, and the barrels took a man as strong as Davidson to handle on road transport.

Earl Friscoe, with some minor schooling to his credit and experience in selling services and supplies, was the brains behind the partnership, and Buckeye Davidson, without a day of schooling to his credit but long service on horseback or with the reins of a wagon team in his hands, was the muscle, the meat, the true shot, the best punch, and one of the most fearless men that Friscoe had ever met.

At the moment, Davidson was healthy, as he'd term it, with the whip for the horses, urging them up an incline in the road that pointed the way to Shiloh Two.

Friscoe, tapping his pal on the shoulder, said, "Don't kill the poor critters, Buck, 'cause they gotta get us home tonight. Even you ain't goin' to pull this load home in place of Blackie up there workin' his tail off. That's a horse, man. He'd be one hellish creature in the corral, I can bet." He shook his head in admiration of the big black horse leading the team of four, part Percheron, part Clydesdale.

"Hell, I wasn't thinkin' any about none a that, 'ceptin' I ain't likin' it too much when we gotta slow down where we could

13

get caught too easy by them maraudin' ones been raisin' all kinds a trouble out here."

He had no sooner gotten that mouthful out of his mouth than the yelling started behind them, and more than a dozen riders in all kinds of costume and gear, saying they were a band of renegades, white, Mexican and possibly Indian, out to get the freighters' load. They were a scurvy looking lot, a few were bare-headed, hats on others as different as their garb, and a variety of weapons in their hands as they pursued the wagon down the road toward Shiloh Two.

Friscoe, with an instant change of caution, said excitedly, "You can hit them critters now, Buck, and get them movin'. Ain't no good standin' still for these kind comin' on us."

"These horses been pullin' us for a spell now, Earl, and maybe I ain't gonna get enough outta them. Any ideas?" He snapped the whip again behind the ears of the lead horse and yelled at him "Go, Blackie. Go, boy. Git a move on, 'cause they's comin' closer."

He turned to Friscoe and said, "Yah didn't answer me, Earl. You got any idea? I'm fresh outta that stuff." He snapped the whip again.

"Yep," Friscoe said, and grabbed the reins from Davidson's hands. "You lay out that unloading plank and hang it off the tail gate and let go a barrel of that good whiskey of Miles's down the ramp of it and see if it slows them down any. Do it so maybe the barrel don't break. Maybe we can get them bozos stoppin' long enough to get drunk'n skunks."

"Miles be mad as hell at the store we lose a barrel of his whiskey," Davidson said, as he stooped into the back of the wagon.

"Buck, if we lose the whole load he'll be madder than Katey Diamond the time we hung her clothes way up in the tree down at the creek. Boy, oh boy, that's some mad. Best let go the barrel when we hit that narrow run up there ahead of us. The loose barrel humpin' on its own might scare a few of them mounts if it goes bouncin' around and rollin' crazy like a drunk on the way through."

Davidson ran a rope around the end of the unloading plank thick as his wrist and hung it off the back end of the wagon after knotting the top end down. The plank bounced a bit but hung in place. He estimated where the wagon was compared to the drop-off point, picked up a barrel with brute effort and swung it

14

sideways on the peak of the bouncing plank. As the wagon ran into the squeeze in the road, he let the barrel slide over the tip of the plank and roll down the plank.

Buckeye Davidson, his eyes lit with glee, a guttural laugh making him feel good, watched as the whiskey barrel hit the ground in a bouncing roll, grazed one hoof of a horse that fell immediately, tossing the rider to the side of the road, and swerving in its travel as it appeared to take aim on others of the gang. To a man the gang drew tight reins and stopped in place, all squeezed into the narrow part of the road.

The barrel of whiskey did not break. The tossed man screamed, "It's a keg of whiskey. A whole keg of whiskey." He yelled halleluiahs enough for the whole gang of them, all gathering swiftly about the barrel, which had finally stopped, intact, on the side of the road.

The two freighters were long gone around the next bend in a matter of minutes. Another mile down the road, sure that they weren't being pursued any longer, Friscoe pulled the wagon off the road and drove it into a small canyon.

"What're ya doin', Earl?" Davidson said, all lit up trying to figure out his partners next planned move. He was sure one was already in place.

"Here's what we do, Buck. We hide the wagon best we can, take the gear off the horses, wait until them critters back there somewhere get good and drunk, and get our stuff back."

"How we do that, Earl?" Davidson felt like scratching his head, but didn't.

"We ride back, slow like, listenin' to drunk sounds, like maybe in an hour or two. They ain't goin' to carry that barrel anyplace, so's they'll drink as much as the can, carry some off, hide some, but get good an drunk in between all that. It's somethin' you'd a come up with, Buck, you give it a bit more pausin'."

A few hours later, the two mounted bareback on the two horses, did not hear the drunken noise first, but saw the glimmer of flames against a canyon wall well off the trail.

Friscoe laid it all out for Davidson. "We gotta get rid of their horses, get as many of their rifles and guns we can, scatter them bozos from here to kingdom come, and get our barrel, whatever's left of it. But them hoot owls ain't made even a big dent in that stuff yet. We'll wait a bit while they get real nasty to one another like they always does."

15

It went as planned, the noise heavier, a few minor squabbles, a few punches thrown, more whiskey poured and drunk. One member of the gang, mad as he could be when posted as a guard, was easy pickings for Davidson an hour later, knocking him into forever with one punch.

The whole crew was deep in sleep, snoring enough to scare away the ghosts. Their rifles and odd side arms were quickly gathered up by the two freighters and hidden among the rocks. The horses, all but two, were allowed to wander out of the canyon. The barrel of whiskey, not even dented as Friscoe had thought, was rolled by Davidson out of the canyon on a slight incline that did not take much energy on his part. He rolled it behind a big rock.

The two partners rode the two captured horses back to the wagon, leading Blackie and his mate by the reins. The pair was hitched back up to the wagon that was driven to where the barrel was loaded back onto the wagon into its same old spot.

The reclamation of their barrel of whiskey had not taken more than six hours after the plot was planned.

The Friscoe-Davidson Freight Co. wagon rode into town, their load almost intact, just enough Old Crow House whiskey siphoned off to get a dozen men drunk enough to fall asleep clean through a sweep of their goods.

At The Lost Mine Saloon that evening, amid the uproarious tales of the two freighters about their escapade, and a constant barrage of comments and questions from the sheriff and Redding of the saloon and Quince of the general store, the sheriff said, "What'd you do with all their weapons? I hate to see them fellas get armed up again in a hurry. Those are the kind you don't hand their guns right back to them after they've been caught nappin'."

Davidson said, "Tucked into that mess of brush about a half mile this side of the last grade. I think they would have tried to get their horses back before they went lookin' for guns. Stuff might still be there, but if they found them horses, coulda found them guns."

Redding said, "You boys did a great job. Drinks on the house, of course, 'cause I'm glad you got through that mess and brought my stuff too. Blackie do his thing?"

"He's pure animal, Miles. Pure animal. Not many like him hereabouts." Friscoe kept nodding his head and everybody knew how much he loved the big black.

16

The sheriff, Abner Baynes, an old timer in Shiloh Two, said, "We'll take a look out that way tomorrow, but I'd best advise you boys to keep a sharp eye come your next trip."

"We'll bust them up again, Abe. They mighta learned already we ain't their pickin's."

"Still," Baynes added, "I'd look over my shoulder all the time. If there's no quit in that gang, like nothing besides liquor gonna slow them down, I'd sure keep the peepers open. But I guess old Blackie'll have something to do for the next trip. Sure is something to look at in the pasture and leadin' the team, that horse."

All of which set an edge in Friscoe, who slipped out for the gents' and went directly to the livery where the team was stabled. He found the owner, Gus Bantry, sitting on a crate and said, "Gus, has anybody been askin' about Blackie and the team, and me and Buck? Like, when are we goin' on our next run?"

"Not yet they ain't, Earl, but I'll keep my eyes and ears open, and let you know anythin' that comes up."

"Thanks, Gus. It don't hurt none to be knowin' stuff like that. Me and Buck will be at Sally's. She moved us into that cabin out back of her place 'cause we're getting' more permanent by the day."

"I'll do that, Earl. You boys did a good job on them skunks. 'Magine, walkin' in on 'em and robbin' from them for a change. Lordie, I love that, and then the sheriff findin' all them guns you boys hid down in the bushes. That was puddin' on the pie far as I'm concerned."

The knock came at the door of the cabin early in the morning two days later, Bantry doing the knocking. "I just had to tell you boys one gent's been watchin' me move around and exercise the horses for two days now. And anytime I walk Blackie out there, he scoots off and comes back with another gent. I seen 'em both around a bit lately, but don't know them. They watch me and Blackie like we was a pair of prizes at the fair. I think that's payin' attention that needs some payin' attention to." His smile was as wide as the brim on his hat.

"That's great stuff, Gus. We're gonna set some stuff up for them, me and Buck and the sheriff. It's better to beat them with our game than try them at their game. We mighta been awful lucky that whiskey barrel wasn't empty in the first place."

17

The next morning, dawn barely with a grip on the day, Blackie and the team was hitched up to the canvas shrouded wagon by Bantry and a helper as it sat beside the livery. The team was a formidable looking team and Blackie looked like he could draw the wagon up the nearest mountain. He also looked like he could outlast the day itself.

When Friscoe and Davidson showed up, the two men bristled with pride at the sight of the team all hitched up and ready to go, and Blackie looking like a statue to horseflesh.

"Ain't he the sight," Friscoe said, and in an aside, said to Bantry, "That gent been around this mornin', Gus?"

"Yup," Bantry said. "He run off as soon as he saw me hitch the team to the wagon, then I saw him and another rider head out of town, goin' east."

"We'll let you know how it goes, Gus, providin' we can," Frisco said as he mounted the wagon and took the reins, Davidson climbing up beside him like a man of the mountain.

Six miles out of Shiloh Two, in a tight twist in the road, five riders flashing handguns in the air ordered the freighters to stop the wagon.

One rider, masked, appearing to be the leader, said, "You boys think you're pretty damned smart, but we come to get our guns back, all of them. Where'd you stash 'em?"

"You wanted us should have sat on our thumbs while you robbed us?" Friscoe said. "Ain't no sense at all in throwin' good guns away."

"Well, where are they?"

"We got 'em all here, right in the wagon," Friscoe said.

"Let's have 'em back then," the bandit said.

"Alright," Davidson said as he snapped back the canvas and a dozen rifle-armed men of a silent, horseless posse sat there in the bed of the wagon with their rifles pointed at the bandits. The sheriff stepped down from the wagon, his pistol aimed at the gang leader, and said, "You and all your boys best drop your guns right now."

The soft thuds sounded in quick succession as gun belts hit the ground. The sheriff, after putting manacles on the gang members and five of his posse taking the bandits' horses for the ride back to town, the others as guards aboard the wagon, said to the freighters, "You boys got some more stories to tell at the saloon tonight. This could get real interesting, you keep this up."

The 2ⁿᵈ Dead Horse Saloon

It sits at the fork of a river in Texas, The 2ⁿᵈ Dead Horse Saloon, and at a fork in the road. Water and wherever go two ways at once whenever you get here and look around. The name of the town is Bapst and there's nobody who knows where that name came from, at least not living here now.

But the owners of the saloon in Bapst are two solid-looking men, Stocker Breslin and Stuart Holmes, one an easterner who went west and the other, a northerner who went south. They met in an unfair gunfight on the trail, each immediately from two directions sticking up for an out-manned and out-gunned lone target they observed under heavy gunfire and pinned into his last retreat.

They made the difference from their cover, driving two thugs off the road, leaving two others as dead as one of Breslin's mackerels or one of Holmes' shooting-back-at-a-Mountie fugitives. In both cases, both goners. They had a good look at the bushwhackers, who had not seen either one of them, Breslin or Holmes, the saviors of the moment and hidden from full sight.

The rescued man, though sorely and vitally wounded, and bleeding so as to say no saving would rear its hope, was Joshua Nettles, who asked for "a pencil quick" to write a note. Luckily, Holmes had a 2-inch stub of a pencil in the band of his hat. The note, as it turned out, was Nettle's last word on worldly matters and gave his rescuers half each of a saloon he had won in a card game, but advised that he was set upon by cohorts of the former owner who lost his ownership when he put down the deed as collateral in a big pot. Nettle's quick note was added to the deed.

"It's called The Dead Horse Saloon. It's in Bapst, down the trail a ways in west Texas, where I was just heading to after looking for my daughter in a few towns out this way, but all that's on this paper."

He coughed one more tell-tale cough both men recognized, each of them having been in enough battles to know the sound of death, the sneak coming up on a man even if he was looking right at it.

"You best do me honor, gents, and if my daughter ever shows up to claim what I should give her, you do the right thing. It has to be this way 'cause I can't let it fall back into the hands of Smoky Woods who just had his men try to take it back from me but you gents took care of that … and her, if she shows up at

19

your door someday. I ain't seen her in a many months 'cause she moves around a lot. Her name's Evelyn but I called her Evie, and she called me Poppa Two 'cause I was her step-father and I love her better than my horse."

He signed the paper, rolled his eyes, said "Evie" like there was a whole bunch of EEs rolled right up front of her name, and made it sound awful sad, like the last thing known by a man who died almost alone in the world.

Breslin and Holmes, by agreement, came into Bapst from different directions and different times, and ended up a few days later as new acquaintances at the bar, Breslin as a come-lately easterner called by the adventures in the west, and Holmes as a lone Montana man looking for new opportunities.

They ended up in the same card game with Smoky Woods, supposed owner of the Dead Horse Saloon.

Talk, also as planned, turned to the saloon, Holmes asking if the saloon business was profitable, and was the place for sale.

Smoky Woods, dealing the hand, said, "Could be it's for sale at the right price." He was a wide-faced man, thick in the neck and brows, leaning all the way into too-heavy in places, let two big rings weigh down his right hand as he dealt the cards, and smiled too often when he was not supposed to smile, like a cougar about to leap from a branch over a rider's head or a high rock alongside the trail. The green in his eyes was sharp as grass just getting a start.

Holmes had seen the type before and discarded the smiles, and the hands seemingly too swift for any normal eyesight, but not the two men sitting as if on command at the next table, their legs free, their hips free, their side arms free and out in the open, the way an easy draw is allowed. They had been sitting like that for days on end, the assignment easy enough to see by people with discerning eyes, like Holmes and Breslin, who fortunately had recognized them from the bushwhacking scene on the trail.

Holmes knew where trouble sat and shifted his eyes so Breslin could note where their interest rested, on the pair of gunmen in place like they had been set there. So Holmes said, "If the price is right and the deed is clear and the bank ain't finding any fault with the paperwork, I'd make an offer for my company to buy it, 'cause we're on the look-out for a foothold down this way, a nice clean start of a new dynasty." His laugh rang around the room, "Course, those gents back there in the company swinging with the money think everything's easy as busting a sick

20

bronc out here, but it ain't. We all know that. Opportunity comes to those who can see it coming down the trail like a runaway wagon."

"With the banker Holdsworth," Woods said, "it always ain't the paper that's the issue, but the word of a good man. Paper stuff don't go too far out here where a man's word is mostly the law among folks of standin'. Holdsworth will do the same if we sell, but you got to come up with a good figure. I'd sell in a flash 'cause I want to go home to the Panhandle for a spell. I ain't been back there in a dozen years and my folks is gettin' on."

Holmes slipped in a few words as he studied his cards. "I'll contact the top dogs and see what they'll give, then we can play around with the figures, with reason of course, and settle it ourselves." He laid down his full house, knowing he had seen the trey of spades before, in the same deal. To himself he admitted, "They are slick as I thought they'd be, even with the cards." He bought his way out of the game with two good losses, even tossing in a pair of aces one time, and said goodnight.

Before the bank opened in the morning, as soon as he saw Holdsworth coming down the street, Holmes met him at the door as he opened it for business. "I have a chance to buy the Dead Horse Saloon, Mr. Holdsworth, and I just want to make sure the paper or the deed is in good fettle for a sale. My company may ask me to get everything in proper order."

"Certainly," Holdsworth said, "it's just business of the day. Now what questions do you have? But if I may volunteer a few facts, it will make everything flow in good order."

His smile was sincere, asking for acceptance the minute it broke wide on his face. "As you must know, out here without lawyers hanging their shingles all over, a man's word is his good bond. That's the situation with The Dead Horse Saloon. It was a man's word and a handshake between Mr. Woods and the former owner, Joshua Nettles, and I was a witness to the sale. It happened only a few months ago. We could do the same thing or I could arrange a deed to be drawn up if the asking price is fair."

Holmes said, "That's real interesting, Mr. Holdsworth. My bosses would probably offer as much as ten thousand for the saloon and the property as it is. I bought a couple of places in East Texas for them not too long ago. They have ideas of a whole bunch of places springing up all over. Kind of dreamy if you ask me, but I only work for them. Would the ten thousand dollar offer interest Mr. Woods?"

"Oh, I am sure it would. How long would it take for you to get the word from your bosses?"

"I'm guessing two or three days, sir. They'd probably send a man with the money. They like to do things that way. It makes things cleaner with cash, don't you agree?"

"That's fine. I'll make the arrangements," the banker said. He stood up and shook hands.

As Holmes was about to leave, he turned to Holdsworth and said, "Just in case Woods is interested, I can make the price a little higher if he might find a way to split the difference with me, if you know what I mean?"

Holdsworth let go with his biggest smile. "I'm sure that would be fine, even at this end with me, if we could make the right arrangements between ourselves, if you understand my position." His smile was right out of a We're-so-much-alike dictionary.

Both men smiled widely, nodded at each other, shook hands again like they had never shook hands before and Holmes walked out whistling a tune he had not whistled in a long while.

Holmes made his way later in the day to the telegrapher and sent off an apparently innocent message, and Breslin kept watch on the telegrapher just in case the banker or Woods made any attempt to find out the contents of the message.

Three days later, a few strangers in town or passing through like normal traffic in a small town, Holmes told a teller at the bank that he'd be back after lunch with his company's agent to take care of the business at hand.

From a position at the livery, Holmes and Breslin and "the company agent" watched at noontime as the banker walked off to the saloon and came out twenty minutes later with Woods and the two hired hands recognized as killers of Joshua Nettles.

Holdsworth and Woods entered the bank and the two thugs took up positions outside the bank, each of them at rest and not very cautious. They were flabbergasted when two guns were stuck in their backs and they were ordered down an alley, locked in irons, and taken to the town jail. Neither of them said a word, the hired guns taken with such ease.

Holmes and the company agent stepped into Holdsworth's office a little later and Holmes introduced the agent. "This is the agent I spoke about. His name's Price," which put a big smile on the banker's face as well as on Holmes's, "and he will speak for me and the company."

22

Price appeared as a real steady looking man, with Colts comfortable on his belt, a gray Stetson sitting straight as an arrow on his head, a soft gray vest without a single wrinkle in it, but no smile on his face, and business looming about him like he could buy and sell half the west.

He said, "I've been told that we could possibly do business by handshake as might have been done before with witnesses. If you'd call in a teller or a customer that might be in the bank now, we could get on with this business."

The banker, stepping out of his office saw Breslin in the bank and said, "Sir, would you please step in here and be a witness to some quick business the bank has to close today. I would appreciate it."

"Sure, can," Breslin said, "be my damned pleasure gettin' a view of big business in operation." He laughed an uproarious laugh that bounced off the windows of the bank, and stepped into the office as Holdsworth held the door for him.

Holdsworth said to all those gathered, "We have a witness here and we can do the handshake and get on with business."

Price, standing beside the banker's desk said, his voice full of business with the question of the moment, "Then we are going to do this by handshake with witnesses and with no deed, because one does not exist at the present time?"

"Yes. Sir, that is right. It was a prior handshake with a Mr. Nettles that took care of ownership and we are prepared to do so at this time."

"Then," said Price, with great surprise supposedly riding across his face, "please tell me what this is." Onto the desk he tossed the deed signed over by Nettles to Holmes and Breslin.

The banker almost fainted. Woods went for his gun and was almost to it when Price stuck a gun in his ribs and said, "It'd be my pleasure, Mr. Woods, to provide a response to you, but I'll wait for the law to take care of it."

Woods, knowing it was about to come apart, if it hadn't already, yelled, "Briscoe, Dexter," as loud as he could.

Holmes, as cool as he ever felt, said to Woods, "Them two killers ain't about to come in here to your rescue, Smoky. They're sitting in jail and shooting off their mouths about now how you hired hem to kill Joshua Nettles and try to steal the deed from him that you lost in a card game over in Coster City. He was killed out there on the trail. Me and my pal here are witnesses and we killed two of your bushwhackers and drove you and your pals off and

23

Nettles signed ownership of The Dead Horse Saloon over to us. And Mr. Price here, believe me or not, is the marshal from the territorial office."

Holdsworth, seeing his part in it bigger than it really was, fear leaping around in him like a sick coyote, went for a gun in his desk draw. Price fired one round into the drawer and shattered chunks of it into the banker's lap. The banker collapsed onto his desk, his forehead hitting the desktop with a loud bang, like it was an echo from Price's gunshot.

Holmes, shortly having repainted the sign out front to read "The 2nd Dead Horse Saloon," went on thinking about buying a few more saloons he had thought about earlier, like The 3rd and The 4th and The 5th. Breslin, meanwhile, kept imagining that one day a beautiful blonde, about 24, curvy and luscious and blue-eyed like an angel, would come in the saloon door and walk right up to him and say, "My name is Evie and I've heard some real nice things about you."

The Bridgetown Bard

When the last bridge was built on the Topeka Road, over the Squash River, and a town grew up around the construction site, the laborers called it Bridgetown. Campsites and quickly-built shacks rose abruptly on the nearby grass and in the sudden valley that led down to the river. The workers, of course, after long days at hard labor, slept well, or, after a night of drinking, slept perhaps a bit sounder. Liquor was supplied by a couple of industrious men, in the beginning right from the back of their wagon. And many of the workers did not move on once the community had its growing legs, stretching the walk.

For the first few months there were no lady friends around and entertainment came from cards, rough music in the hands of many real amateurs, and games of man versus man in various frolics of mind and muscle, like checkers and tossing the caber, roping and wrestling, target shooting and poker.

Loneliness, thus, made its continuous way into camp, and into the resultant town now spreading its wings.

A few alert men later remembered the day the lone rider came along the road strumming his guitar, singing songs they had never heard, and riding a mule that moved slower than all-out misery.

"Where you from, Mister? What's that song you're singing? Where did that come from? You from Tennessee? Who wrote that song?" Many of the workers were from "back east a ways" and looked often for any connection to the past they had left for the dreams in the west.

"Well, gents," said the guitar player and singer, still on his mule, "I never sing a song I didn't write myself. My name's Timothy Rains, I never ride the train, conductors never complain, what else can I explain?"

Reining back on his mount, he immediately broke into another song; "I'm coming down the ramp into the Bridgetown camp, my horse is itchin' for some oats and my delicious melodious notes that I wrote last night. Those notes I wrote out there in the bare campfire light."

Needless to say, he was cheered on and dared on, "Let's see how fast you can write a song." Those early greeters railed at him to perform. "Do it up. Do it up," they sang and sang.

"Whoa," the bard said. "Hold it. Whoa. A drink I had ain't since school, none for me and my mule. He's dry as bone, I'm

25

without a tone." He laughed and they laughed and the aura was set.

Timothy Rains had made his mark directly on entry into Bridgetown, a one-man band of entertainment and manipulation of the language and a bare knowledge of things musical ... he'd be the first to say he couldn't sing worth a damn, if he was asked, but nobody in Bridgetown, sorely in need of some kind of entertainment, would ever ask a volunteer to explain himself.

Out at the last bridge on the road he gazed, did our hero Rains, seeing the network of timbers as they criss-crossed and moved upwards in a measured latticework. The bridge was nearly across the river, its feet now firmly planted on both sides of the river but not completely joined yet, a broad and magnificent reach speaking loudly about planning, daring, commitment to a task, the hard work by all hands ... hands who must be entertained, and thus literally "milked" of their few dollars, a poor trade off if they were ever to be asked ... but nobody taking in the coin would ever ask for an explanation.

Rains, on first sight of the wagon dispensing liquor, squirreled the two owners into a quick conversation, swung a deal with both men, cornered a piece of land from a squatter for a few dollars, and put down the first plank on a saloon. It took only a few weeks to build, some of the lumber and supplies mysteriously coming available in hours of darkness, obviously from railroad supplies meant for the bridge and ongoing construction work.

But the first, original and only saloon ever allowed in Bridgetown, The Bridgeworkers Bar and Grill, began its two-year reign of existence on the far side of the bridge. Timothy Rains, chief proprietor, barkeep, waiter, song and dance man, sole entertainer for long months, ran a tight shop where coin was considered. It was this activity that prompted him to propose a bank to be built in town "to hold in account the good business success of Bridgetown." Of course, it was to be built as an annex to his current property, The Bridgeworkers Bar and Grill.

Nothing but success at business and his strange talents set Rains aside as "different" in the community. All else with him was the same as the eager men locked into dreams of the golden nugget, the big find, the elusive female companionship that all the townsfolk clung to.

Life for Rains went sweeping along as the saloon did a grand business, the bank opened, and the bridge, nearing final completion, brought a flurry of activity into the area. The basic

26

core of that flurry was the arrival of a blonde woman with oriental cheekbones, eyes blue as a grand sky, and a robust figure that caught the eyes of every man in Bridgetown, especially the eyes of the town's leading citizen. When he first saw Geraldine Malden his heart leaped like it had never leaped. A song wanted to come to his mouth, but it never made its way out of his chest. It was the first real announcement that life for him, as he had known it, had ultimately changed.

"Mr. Rains," she said as she walked up to him standing in front of the saloon, now four times its original size and a floor taller, "I am Geraldine Malden and I understand that you have rooms upstairs. I would like to rent one for some weeks, if that is possible, but it has to be a nice room and not any flea-littered tract of wasteland, like some of the places I have seen and never dared enter for a night."

Her hand in his hand was the softest thing he had touched since a baby rabbit had quivered in his hands out on the prairie, and it put an attractive halting into his voice. "Of course, Ma'am," he said, "the best room in the house is yours."

"Why thank you, Mr. Rains, but I would have assumed that you had the best room in the house," Her eyes flashed wickedly, but with a reigning innocence that stayed with him.

"It was my room indeed, Ma'am, but now it is yours. It shall be made up to suit you in a few hours. In the meantime, may I treat you to dinner in the saloon, in the restaurant part, of course?" We know, of a certainty, that all rhyme and reason had gone away in a hurry. He could not rhyme two words in an instant if he was bent over backwards … the words just did not come to him.

It was a romance of the ages, of the era, of the growing west, and Rains worked harder than ever to make business better than even he had dreamed of. The pair, loving lovebirds to all onlookers, made the romance one of gayety and color, and any free moment he would drive her in a carriage to show her the area around Bridgetown. When the first engine, without any cars attached to it, sort of a test run, passed over the bridge, a huge celebration took place. Rains threw open the bar for a solid two hours, "as long as the day's supply lasts," he said in his announcement. Then he added, "I will say now that the first passenger and freight train is due here two days from now, on Monday of the week, and we'll have a real celebration, a daylong that Bridgetown will remember forever." He smiled at Geraldine standing at the head of the stairs, as beautiful as he had ever seen her.

It was such moments as this one, seeing how she could burst a day wide open by just standing still in one place, that he wished he could make up a song for her, sing the words like he had never sung before, let her know he was hers completely.

Geraldine smiled at him as if she was reading his thoughts. She sent that slight, subtle flirtatious nod and eye move, almost a wink, down to him that cut through to his heart. If he could not write a song for her at that moment, he'd never be able to write a song. In effect, he accepted that agreement as though no words would make any difference in how he felt about her.

She managed a wave of one hand that was just as subtle and just as inviting when she turned back to her room in the front of the building and disappeared from sight. There was a sudden emptiness above him, a place that lost its immediate luster in a fraction of a second. He couldn't believe the sudden loss, how the general surroundings went away with her, all the things that he thought he saw, thought he knew, and thought were real.

At that moment, the teller of the bank, and his accounting specialist, Joel Wardlin, approached him and said, "Boss, we got to put some of this money in the vault. This is one of the best days we've ever had, and Smithson at the general store said the same thing to me just now. He's almost at a selling-out point and expects his new load of supplies to come in on the train tomorrow. Says he better put it in the vault too. He also said he saw a few new faces in town today and yesterday and is a bit nervous. I told him I'd speak to you, but all I saw have been a few new prospectors bound for the hills above us and those bare dreams we all have."

"Go ahead, Joel," Rains said, still locked onto the memory of Geraldine's image as she turned away, the shine in her hair, the movement of her body, the little wave of her hand the way a sworn secret is carried out in full view of the world. "You do what you think you have to do, Joel. You're a good man at the job. But I have something to tell you; some of the ladies have been calling you 'the handsome dog who hides all the money in town.' Some of them, for sure, are bound to have their eye on you, Joel. You best watch your tail before you get caught up in it all."

"That isn't always bad, is it, Boss?" His smile was as wide as the river, or the bridge that crossed it.

28

That night the blast went off. It was near 2 o'clock in the morning, Monday morning, the morning after a full celebration and another day of it coming along. Some people never heard a sound, but some, like Rains, scrambled from bed wondering where the loud sound had come from. A few men rushed into the street and a fusillade of shots greeted them from too many corners worth counting, or noting. They scrambled back to their protective surrounding, any wall was protection for the moment.

One man had cried out as a bullet hit him in his thigh, and Rains, never thinking about the bank, only about Geraldine up in her room, rushed around to get a gun, any gun, preferably a rifle that was lodged for emergencies under the bar.

It was not there. Nor was the barkeep's pistol, supposedly lodged in the same spot. Some alert person, he couldn't figure who, had beaten him to it. Forces, at least, were at work.

Panic hit him. He thought about the bank. Disbelieved his thought. Nobody in town would dare rob his bank. In a brief second he forgot about the bank and remembered Geraldine alone upstairs, exposed to gunfire and what else might come along.

In a mad-long dash he reached the stairs and started to climb them. More gunfire rang out, sounding as if it was coming from the back of the building instead of the front, where it had started. Still in a panic about Geraldine's safety, he jammed his shoulder against the door of her room, not knocking as she had demanded right from the very beginning. The door burst open as he jammed his whole body at it.

The room was empty.

Geraldine was not there.

He glanced at her bureau. He saw nothing. The drawers were empty. The small closet was empty.

She was gone. Geraldine was gone. The love and light of his life was gone. More gunfire ensued when he looked out her window down onto the main street. It was as though they were shooting directly at him. He ducked low, looked around again, and rushed down the stairs.

One of the old faithful customers, a drunk if you'll have it, was sitting at the bar, a full bottle at hand.

Rains yelled at him. "Have you seen Geraldine? She's not upstairs. Have you seen her?"

The drunk, topsy-turvy if ever he was, said, "Last I saw of her, before the shooting, her and Joel were going in the door of the bank. He's that good lookin' one that works for you, you know

29

the one I'm talkin' about? The good lookin' one all the ladies talk about?" He poured himself another full shot of whiskey, oblivious of his surroundings.

Rains fled the saloon, heading to the bank.

There was a silence suddenly in the air. The general store owner, Smithson, stood beside him, and said, "They hit the bank, Tim. Blew the door off the vault, swept everything out of there and fled down the street and across the bridge on a hand car, five of them, going like hell across the bridge. We're getting a posse together right now. I got a horse coming for you."

"I can't go now. I have to find Geraldine. She's not up in her room. I looked. There's nothing there. I have to find her before she gets hurt." He turned to go somewhere.

Smithson said, a halting in his voice, "She's with them, Tim." He had a sheepish look on his face.

"Is she hurt?" Rains said. "Is she being held hostage? I'll give them anything, everything I've got."

"She's part of them, Tim. Her and Joel are the bosses, from what it looks like to me. The livery boy said he heard her giving orders, said he heard her say, 'We have to get to the other side of the bridge as soon as we can. Once we get over there, the way the river's rushing mad, we have a great chance to get away with everything.'"

"No!" yelled Rains. "Not Geraldine. Not my Geraldine." The panic was full bore. "We have to get over there, find out the truth."

"Here comes your horse, Tim. We'll go look now, see what's what. My money was in the bank too. Now it's all gone. Every penny of it."

They mounted their horses as the hastily-gathered posse reined up in front of them.

The whole troop of the posse, Rains in the rushing lead, were almost at the entrance to the bridge when the second explosion of the night went off. The blast filled the night with a thunderous flash of light, accompanied by a sound as if a monster bomb had exploded, and a huge chunk of the brand new Bridgetown Bridge went clattering tumbling into the rushing waters of the river.

Timothy Rains, entrepreneur, maker of rhymes, song writer and entertainer, once a saloon owner and a banker, felt the music in his throat, at his lips.

He waited for the words to tumble loose.

30

The Dam at Wasahoa

The settlement of Wasahoa in the Utah Territory sat on the Wasatch Plateau and was ripe with game. This cool forest high above the San Rafael Swell provided refuge for an incredible amount of prey, which also included all manner of criminals on the run, from all over the western region. One establishment in Wasahoa was reserved for bank robbers only, the owner figuring her clients were able to spring with cold cash. Her name was Masi Begoyne, widowed three times by the law of the posse. When it was decided to dam waters flowing from the Wasatch Plateau the plan in the very beginning meant to include the San Rafael and San Pitch Rivers and Muddy Creek.

Masi Begoyne wanted no part of it, liking her situation and things as they were: her in control of seen and unseen properties and such assets. As she was heard to say a few times, "I've earned what I've got and I'll keep what I've earned, and all to myself unless there's a better man out there than the last three I've had as my husbands. Each of them got caught and killed. I'm tired of being widowed."

She set her eyes on William Tawonda Brody, engineer of the new dam project, and she did not feel the slightest twinge when she fixed him up with a room at her "small digs I got by scratching for them." Masi had 12 rooms at Her Place, above Her Saloon where the painting of "Her" stood mural-wide behind the bar in the saloon, a resplendently reclined, hand-gestured painting of a woman with nothing more than she was born with adorning her frame. At least once each weekend a tipsy drinker, leaning back and forth with his day-dreams rocking him, fell to the floor and had to be dragged outside. Masi saw to it that they would not be robbed by holding their money "until he comes back to collect it." Very often, when they woke, they never realized their money was missing, and so did not pursue the situation.

Brody was as handsome as Masi was good-looking, and each felt a spark of inner recognition at the first meeting. "I hear you own the hotel and the saloon among other local property, Miss Begoyne is it?" His voice and his eyes carried the answer to what he had asked. "I'm looking for quarters for my stay here in Wasahoa during the planning of the dam project. When it kicks off, when money is arranged, there will be lots of traffic, lots of workers in the mix."

His eyes said other results would also be at hand.

31

Nonplussed, Masi looked him right in the eye and replied, "I am the mistress of my own fate, Mr. Brody, and I gather you are a gentleman and a scholar of fine tastes." She paused, made a subtle gesture of innocence, and said, "I have a room for you, on the corner with a view of the street and of the whole range as you look at it," at which declaration she advised her bartender to "go clean out that room including the current tenant."

Brody moved in, set up his office in a corner of the room where he looked down on the street and up at the range where millions of gallons of water gathered annually and which he wanted to bring unto the dam planned for Wasahoa.

The dam was not a dream, not a feather-brained scheme to draw and drag funds out of rich eastern pockets, though he realized the full possibility of such a scheme. He'd do his end, and worked hard in his study to draw up the best plan possible: he would get the water caught, trained, and aimed.

His nights, of course, had other potential, further pursued when Masi suggested that the dam was really not the best thing for this part of the country, at least not where he had planned to collect the water, in the Canyon of Dark Caves.

"Bill," she said one night in her sultriest voice, her face rouged, her lips red, her dress fitting her with practiced precision, tightened where necessary, loose where not, "I own a good piece of the backside of the canyon. Bought it off a miner a few years back, Moses Denby, when he fell ill and I set him up here in this very room, to last out his final days. Moses signed his claim over to me, winked at me and said 'Don't treat it light, Masi. Don't treat it light.' Those were almost his last words. Then, in a last gesture, he pointed to his teeth. I could not figure that out for the longest time, but finally I realized Moses had found gold, had made a gold strike. He told me without mentioning a word. I just know it was gold teeth he was saying, in other words like they say. I've never told a soul about it until you. It has to be protected."

"Well," Brody said with an interesting tone, "maybe we out to take a ride out there tomorrow and see what's what. We should know without any doubt about what you're holding onto."

She placed a conciliatory hand on his shoulder.

In the morning, the sun about to fly up, loose from the Wasatch Range, the engineer and "Her" of "Her Place" rode out of town on a pair of palominos a painter would love to see, twins, genetic parts showing in a matched trot, colors waiting for dawn to touch and go happy on, pride in a pair.

In the morning sun the pair climbed up slow inclines at the beginning of the range and entered a long, deep canyon whose cliff faces were marked with the darkness of cave mouths. Near the base of one sheer cliff, as if tossed there in prehistoric times as a mere shadow, was the small black mouth of an entrance that led to a long cave on one side which was found a tunnel dug for about 30 feet. At the end of the tunnel the two adventurers found a boulder that obviously had been rolled inside the tunnel from outside the cave and then set in place against the tunnel wall.

Brody realized what it was, but Masi had no idea, except it was a sign left her by Moses Denby.

When Brody, with some engineering with a heavy pole found outside, moved the boulder, another depression came visible. He lit a torch to get a better look, saw with deep surprise what some men have looked a lifetime for, a diagonal, downward sweeping streak in the wall of a gold strike, a shining strata of promised riches. The breath caught in his throat, and he pulled Masi close to him, his strong arms around her soft form. She kissed him as if she knew what he was about to say. She thought it would be together, get all the supplies you'll need, hire me as your engineer, and open your own filthy rich mine. This might be the strike of strikes. All that has to be done is make sure the dam doesn't get in the way of things."

She kissed him again. Does that bother you?"

"Of course, the kiss does," he smiled, and kissed her back, "but I have a problem with the dam. I signed a contract and it is bounden on me."

"Would it bother you if someone other than you broke the binding of that contract?" She could still feel the sweet pressure of his arms around her, and the lingering tone of a promise that could hang all of it out to dry in the wind, and then get blown away plain as tumbleweed in the rush to nowhere.

"If someone up the chain of command, like at the top of the whole shooting match, was to break the contract, I'd follow that too, right to the break up."

Masi settled into his arms and said, "I hope something like that happens for you." She closed her eyes when she kissed again, thinking of his nearness and all the possibilities abroad in the land.

The official layout of the dam was finally drawn up after weeks of land and water flow measurement, all options regarded or disregarded after study, and the project presentation was ready for the top dogs, the big money from back east. Brody was confident the presentation would be okayed, and a whole range of thoughts hit him. Foremost was Masi and how she ended up if all of it went through. He was in his room of the hotel waiting for the big contact, who was Sir Arthur Trainor of the Allied Pacific and Atlantic Railroad and Utilities Company. Trainor was due in with his department heads … and his family, all going to wrap business and a vacation in the mix before they'd return to New York.

Trainor, as would be seen in a hurry, was a land-rich, silver spoon heir with more chance opportunities than expended effort, who came easily to his gains. He was also a bright man who had seen well beforehand the impact of railroads crossing the new country now moving explosively west quicker than the crown changed hands, or heads. With an alertness grown from observation and a certain feel for things mundane, like money, he had always made sweet gains.

Two stage coaches brought the parties into Wasahoa in the late afternoon, and dropped them off at Masi's hotel, all rooms but Brody's vacated for them. Trainor's wife and two daughters were in one room, Trainor in a room by himself, and his party split out in the other rooms. Masi kept her eyes on all the members of Trainor's entourage from her spot at the end of the bar, catering to Mrs. Trainor and her daughters as if she had been a maid in their home and was on vacation with them. Trainor, as late evening progressed, and his family retired to their room, found himself alone with Masi at the bar.

The attractive lady of the west intrigued him from the first sight, the way she carried herself, the imminent danger that lurked about her person, the live animal she portrayed, all grabbed Trainor by the lapels and hauled him in.

Masi, as planned, looked her very best, all dolled up in a dress that showed what might not be seen in another dress, and Trainor was all eyes for her somewhat subtle display. When Trainor mounted the stairs with her and went to his room, three employees stood outside the room in semi-darkness until they heard Masi say, in a louder voice than regular, "Well, now, look at this."

They stepped into the room, saw Masi stripped of her dress, blood dripping from her nose, and Sir Arthur Trainor standing beside her, holding her by one arm."

34

"What's going on here, Masi?' one of her employees said, "Are you okay, Masi? What's this guy been doin' to you?"

Trainor, old hand at situations, recognized everything at once. Looking over his shoulder to the next room where his family was quartered, he said, "All right, here. What's the deal? What are you looking for? I can see with easy discernment that I am caught up in extenuating circumstances having a certain aroma hovering over them." He looked at Masi, still nude ass ever, and said, "Is Brody a participant in this farce?"

Masi, flipping her dress back on her form, said, "Not in any way. He's been working his butt off to get this damned dam built for you regardless of what I wanted, and I want him as much as anything. The dam is secondary. I never loved a man like him. As you can see, I'd do anything for him, but not let the dam get built. That would just spoil everything for us. He's an honest man, the kind I haven't met in a while, but we have other expectations."

"Well," Trainor said, "providing that my wife hears nothing about this and none of my associates, all sound asleep at this hour, I can guarantee the dam will not be built at Wasahoa."

He winked at Masi and added, "You are a most attractive woman, and he's a lucky man. But we weren't going to erect any dam out here in the middle of nowhere. Not even in the first place. This was more a planned vacation than anything else. An inside request, if you know what I mean," and he again looked over his shoulder at his family's room.

"What do you suggest my family ought to see tomorrow, what good sites in the area? Is there a cattle drive on the horizon? A duel between fast guns?"

"Not yet," Masi said, "but I can arrange anything you want. Anything at all."

Trainor, opening the door so they could leave, said, "I don't doubt that one bit, my dear."

He patted her on her backside as she left the room, her perfume hanging in the air, ripe as an adieu never to be forgotten.

35

Jehrico's Wolf Pup

When Jehrico's wolf pup bit the sheriff, on his gun hand, and on his trigger finger to boot, things went from bad to worse. To begin with, Ruben Tarpon was a new sheriff with a fast gun and was trying his best to make his name as good as his gun and do a good job for the folks of Bola City. He was also checking out the pup as a curiosity, some folks telling him about it locked in a cage behind the livery. The sheriff had heard about Jehrico's stunts and ventures into the business side of Bola City, like his hauling in the first iron bath tub to serve the hygienic needs of Bola City's male population. Jehrico, Tarpon figured, was gifted with accidental entrances into things that made him money, and him being nothing more than a collector of odd things found in his travels, often just junk. Jehrico, however, knew firsthand the desert, older Indian sites and dwelling areas, ghost towns, closed-down mines, caverns and caves and canyons, and the community trash deposits for a hundred miles around that he reveled exploring in.

None of that stopped the bite when the sheriff put his hand too close to the pup.

And the bitten finger had a far-reaching effect on Bola City's relationships between the law, local merchants, and the bank.

The sheriff, an elected official, said aloud to some confederates, "This is all the fault of that damned junk collector, him and his pup." Though he was a stalwart among the men and a favorite of the women with his ruggedly handsome looks, he was aware of his status at all times, knowing it all came with the territory of the badge, the turn of a key to a jail cell, and the hangman's noose when it counted.

It all had begun so simply for Jehrico in his newest venture into the world of collecting things. He came up with the pup at the back end of a cave in the mountains, born to snarl it appeared, but cute as a doll.

"Look for the dog in him, Jehrico. He's as much dog as anythin'." Jehrico's pal Joe Brewster was laying it on the line about Jehrico's new wolf pup he'd brought to Brewster to get his view on having one for a pet. Brewster knew animals, once having lived in the hills around the Strict Elsie settlement on the Guila River for at least ten years before he walked out of the hills

36

one day and came to town of Strict Elsie, leaving all the genuine silence behind him.

He'd spotted Jehrico as soon as he cleared the pass at the high point above Strict Elsie, some vultures riding the thermals hundreds of feet above him, their wings, even that far, as wide as the back side of a pair of oxen in the traces. It was not until Jehrico came within fifty yards that Brewster knew he was carrying a bundle of fur. The way he carried it told Brewster the fur was alive and, of course, had to be a young one.

"Watcha got there, Jehrico? It's near alive far as I kin see. It ain't peccary and it ain't cow, so I'd guess it's gotta be bear or wolf, and if you say it's wolf, make sure you handle it like a dog. Like I said, it's much dog as anythin'."

He shook his head and said, "If you bring it down into Bola City, be ready to get some sand in your grits; them folks down there don't like anythin' that even smells wolf. So best tell 'em up front it's a dog you found with the momma dead. Them big male wolves have been nosin' into the wind for a hundred years now. It travels on the breeze, in the wind, and if they find it like we do comin' in from a month in the desert, knowin' girl on the wind from a hundred miles away, they'd get mean at things plumb near forgot."

Jehrico, all smiles, still holding the pup like he was a toy, ignoring the threats of real life, said, "What'll I call him, Joe? Got any special names you ain't used up yet? I favor south names, if you know what I mean."

Brewster, looking at the vultures still at games, said, "How about Bruto, him bein' so mean and all? Bruto's good name for that critter just waitin' to bite your finger off given a chance he come of age." The two old pals laughed long and loud as they shared the bundle of fur, with white teeth in the middle of the ball.

"You keep to mind them teeth, Jehrico, 'cause they come to growin' easy as the ground shakin' when the mountain moves. Bruto get set to use them there's no kiddin' around on him. Them kind ain't born to chew, I should tell you. They was plain born to rip things apart, one part from another, 'specially they any meat in between or settin' on them parts."

The two friends of the animal world set about to make a cage for Bruto, after Jehrico poured some water from his canteen on the pup and said, "I bless you and give you the name Bruto. Wear it where you will, but for now in this here cage we got made,

37

me and Joe. It's just to keep you from the dogs in town, and there's lots of them nosin' around all the time."

Brewster added a bit more advice. "You best let Bruto smell you every time you feed him, Jehrico. Let him get your smell down good in his belly 'cause it might save a finger or a hand later he come of real age and them teeth do the real thing."

Jehrico had a rig behind his mule that he could tote the cage in, and that's how they entered Bola City, Jehrico on his mule and the wolf pup in his cage.

For starters, the sheriff was practically out of commission, and most people around knew it, including some gang members sitting in a cabin at the back end of Snake Canyon off in the mountain range, and knowing the hand of the law was bandaged to a fare-thee-well.

"He ain't so good a shot anymore," Dutch the German said, talking to his small gang of robbers, all rested after their last robbery, and just about all the money spent. "He ain't going to get the jump on us, his hand like it is. That damned wolf pup did us a great big favor. Bola City's next for us, boys, and that bank over there. We ought to give a toast to that scrounger that brought home a wolf pup, thinking he was going to fool people making them think it was a lost puppy dog his momma run off or killed."

One member of the gang, No-Foolin' Toulin, at the back end of the cabin, whittling on a stick, said, "We gotta have a better plan than last time, Dutch. We was lucky on that one." He rolled his eyes and flashed his hands in the air, both moves for base punctuation.

"Whatta ya mean 'we was lucky?'" said Dutch. "We came out of there with a whole satchel of dough. So we lost Butchie. Well, he ain't no big loss to us. You gotta admit he screwed up on the Timberfield job and I think he was asleep again this time. No way he shoulda taken one right in the face. Just wasn't payin' attention and somebody else coulda been dropped too, in case you ain't thought of that yet." He stressed his statement by pointing to each one in turn and saying, "You or you or you and even you. All of you coulda had the deep end of the tunnel all to hisself, if you really think about it."

A small wave of mumbling ensued and Dutch the German knew none of the others would speak up; they were too scared, but Toulin came right back. "That stupid scavenger, that Jehrico lug, he ought to be part of us, way things happen with him. You heard about his bath tub and his pianer he brought back one time,

38

like the whole world turned over on its backside for him. They say he smells like gold or silver up close and even gets a free bath once a week. Man like that could throw a whole passel of Rangers right off our trail, he give it a mind to do so."

Dutch the German had a sudden idea, and he let it run around in his head before he spoke up about it. "What about this?" he said, leaning forward, looking them in the eye, drawing them in one by one. "We turn that wolf pup loose. Let him shake up a few folks, the whole town maybe, and while the pup raises hell of any kind, we rob the bank when they're all messed up with the thing being loose, like maybe he's gonna bite a kid or some old lady hangin' up clothes on her line, or just layin' around like nothin' ever's gonna happen, but the sheriff hisself is already punched out of action by a baby wolf."

"He still keep that pup behind the livery, near the tub set-up?" No-Foolin' Toulin obviously knew the answer to his own question. "Want I should take care of him, Dutch? I ain't too queasy doin' somethin' like that." His head came down into the circle where Dutch's head had been, demanding attention, getting it, along with a share of responsibility and command. Smiling at Dutch, and then at the other gang members, he laid out a plan. "I figure I ought to feed him somethin' good, what he likes, while he's still in the cage. If he's on the running line, loose as far as his leash lets him go, I'll still feed him with that somethin' goin' to get his blood all lathered up inside, waitin' to bite the hell out of anybody else comes near him. I learned a trick from an old Indian one time, about dropping a piece of meat in a special sauce, makes an animal go kinda crazy he eats it."

"Sounds pretty smooth, No-Foolin'," Dutch said. "He scare half the women in town to screamin' and we got a walk-through at the bank, and Sheriff Tarpon ain't gonna draw down on us no way, while all the men folk try to be heroes for their women and kids."

It all went awry, of course, by the intervention of, not by Jehrico himself, but by his pal, the joker and animal man, Joe Brewster, who, during the darkest part of the night, extricated the wolf pup from the cage, put him in a box in the loft of the livery, and inserted a badger in its place. The badger was as mean as possible for one his size, and Brewster was just hoping to have some fun come morning.

He got all he was looking for.

39

In the forenoon of the day, a full night's sleep behind him, Jehrico came to feed the pup and was surprised, but not amazed, to see an entirely different critter in the cage. Instinctively he knew that Brewster had been afoot in the night. He decided not to show any anxiety or any of his surprise, because he wanted to set off Brewster in his own way. The critter was a new one to Jehrico and he decided not to feed him, just to get back at his pal and omit what might be an exciting moment. He heard the wolf pup up in the livery and went to check on him and to feed him his morning ration.

Of course, the exciting moment came when an unsuspecting and usually morning-sleepy No-Foolin' Toulin came to initiate his plan to feed the wolf pup and set him free to raise havoc all around Bola City. He did not pay much attention to the critter and when he opened the cage to toss in his "special food supply," that all-out mean badger latched onto the ankle of his boot with a grip that was not about to loosen and sent No-Foolin' Toulin in a mad, wild, screaming escapade all around the livery area. He wanted desperately to shoot the critter but he could not get his handgun free of his holster, falling knocked down repeatedly or getting knocked against a wall and further drawing out from his deepest insides the unholiest of screams.

Those screams swept across the morning of Bola City like a wild animal caught in a deadly snare, which did force the actions of an uncounted number of people within hearing range.

Jehrico thought it to be Brewster getting hung up in his own tomfoolery, Dutch the German and his gang thought it to be the outcome of the wolf pup on the loose, as promised by Toulin, and Sheriff Tarpon thought someone was being attacked by thugs or a wild thing inside the town limits.

Jehrico sat back in the loft laughing his head off, the wolf pup locked under a box with a heavy weight on top of it. Dutch the German and his gang rushed into the bank to rob it. Sheriff Ruben Tarpon grabbed a pistol in his left hand and fired a shot in the air, then fired another shot, in his attempt to scare off any wild critter or a thug on his rounds of doing nothing good, whatever was going on in his town.

When No-Foolin' Toulin rolled out into the main street of Bola City, the badger let go of Toulin's leg and rushed towards the bank in his attempt to escape. Some women screamed their holy terror. People on the wooden walk, which ran in front of the bank and the general store, rushed into the open doors of both

40

establishments, spilling goods in the store and throwing the bank hold-up into absolute turmoil with every man in the place wielding a gun, some expecting to rob the bank and some expecting the wild critter to come right through the front door and were ready to shoot him.

Sheriff Tarpon ran into the street with the smoking pistol in his left hand and screaming all the while for his deputy to get on the job.

Jehrico stayed in the loft, the wolf pup under wraps, envisioning what pal Joe Brewster might be thinking at the time, all the screams and the gunfire and the general excitement gathering steam in the middle of town.

To his credit, pal Joe Brewster was on his horse outside of town heading back to Strict Elsie, hearing the gunshots, thinking that somebody in Bola City was taking shots at the badger out and about town, thinking of Jehrico looking for the wolf pup all the while, and he himself counting ahead to all the laughs they'd have next time him and Jehrico got together, away from Bola City, probably during one of Jehrico's scavenger hunts.

The Barber's Romance

For the longest time in the short history of Bullfront, Colorado, Clark Goodrich's most prized possession was his barber chair, hauled west from St. Louis, Missouri in 1876 by his father, a barber before him. The chair, the first of its kind ever seen by his father, had been abandoned when it was found in the barn of a barber friend. But it was not a complete chair. With a bit of his own ingenuity, the elder Goodrich completed the chair so it could swing in a circle and, with use of two levers, was able to be swung back to a nearly prone position. It was the centerpiece of the barbershop in Bullfront.

When his father was killed by a stray bullet in an argument on the main street of Bullfront, Clark Goodrich became the sole owner of the small shop and the special chair. Business was good and life for the barber moved along in its casual manner in the bustling western town. Mining for gold and silver proceeded in the mountains and streams, cattle for big markets was raised out on the grass, and commerce moved placidly on the river. The railroad would come in a few years. The barber's chair was the only one of its kind in the general area around Bullfront.

Then came the day, Friday business bristling on the first day of summer, when Widow Maggie Collins brought her son Mark in for his summer cut. Mark was four, Maggie was 25 and Goodrich was 32 by two days.

Life swung into another cycle for the three of them.

For Goodrich, it was love at first sight, his eyes setting on the beautiful blonde in a blue dress, pink cheeks and red lips that glistened with moisture. Her eyes leaped with blue abounding her. His eyes then set on a window placard announcing a dance in a few weeks; love began to work its ways into position.

For Maggie's part in the small drama, she noted at first how carefully the barber treated Mark sitting high on the chair on an extra board, which warmed her, and how neat the barber's hair was, making him as attractive as any man she had noticed since her husband was killed two years earlier by rustlers. As a result of her husband's death she had sold the ranch a year earlier and moved into town, buying a small house on the edge of Bullfront where it faced the mountains. The house had a porch with two comfortable chairs, two flower boxes by the porch windows, and a small garden at one side.

42

Goodrich knew all about her husband's death, as all news seemed to pass through the barbershop as much as it did the saloon or the general store or the front of the church after Sunday meeting, or in the pages of the town weekly newspaper, "The Purple Sage." The barber often imagined himself in the place of some of the characters whose stories spun through his shop. But he had the ability to cut short any of those daydreams that might make life move in another realm.

When Maggie Collins brought Mark back for a second cut less than a month later, Goodrich knew an interest had been kindled with the young widow. He took extra good care of Mark sitting high on the chair and managed to slip him a candy near the end of the cut. The boy smiled his thanks, his mother patted the barber on the shoulder on parting, and Goodrich was deeper in love than ever.

A week later, as slow as life is in some towns, and with some people, he saw her again in the store and asked if he could call on her as they talked in the corner of the store. She said yes, and the arrangements were made.

As much as Goodrich was in love, and Maggie Collins seemed to dote on the idea of having a man around, a man who paid attention to her and her son, the affair was a slow one. Goodrich, never rushed while working the clippers or scissors, didn't rush at romance either. Comfort set in for the two, even as Mark began to depend on the barber for small deeds reserved for fathers of boys.

As it happened in many early western towns, Bullfront received its share of men trying to get rich the easy way. But robbery, proven time and time again, is never easy, for the hounding begins for robbers, and dreams get crushed for others. When the first robbery came affecting our romantic couple, Maggie and Goodrich were gabbing away on his shop porch on a late Friday afternoon, Mark just out from school and talking to a classmate a few feet away.

Shots came from the bank only three doors from the barbershop. Goodrich had just enough time to shove Maggie inside his shop, and turned to look for Mark. The boy and his friend were open-mouthed at the shots and the horses rearing up on hind legs in front of the bank. The sheriff began firing at a man holding two horses outside the bank. The man fired back, and two men ran from the bank with bags of money in their hands. One man also carried a pistol that he began firing wildly about him.

Goodrich, in one leap, swept Mark and his friend into the alley beside the barbershop and thrust them under the building as the gunfire continued. Maggie, trying to run out of the barbershop, was met by Goodrich diving inside while bullets still traversed the whole area.

"Where's Mark," she screamed, grabbing Goodrich by the shoulders, as if she might try to shake the truth out of him.

"He's okay," Goodrich said. "He's underneath us right now. He's out of the way. He's okay." He didn't tell her how Mark had been shoved there.

Maggie Collins dropped her head on the barber's shoulder, a thankful gasp in her breath. Goodrich hugged her.

The robbers had made a getaway with some of the money, one of them hit by a bullet as he rode out of town. Talk was going on about the incident, when the sheriff said, "Maggie, I got to tell you that boy of yours was saved by the barber. He jumped on him and his friend and just about drove both of them under the barbershop, out of trouble's way. Got to thank the man for that."

On the spot, still warm with other feelings for the barber, Maggie Collins kissed Goodrich in front of half the town, even as her son hugged them both.

Goodrich, seizing the moment, said, "Will you go to the dance with me?"

She hugged him back, "Of course I will," she said.

A good part of Bullfront saw or heard about the romance between the barber and the widow Collins, and the romance really blossomed the night of the dance in Tomshek's barn. It all went well, the couple dancing with each other all the time until a drunken cowpoke tried to get too close to Maggie. That's when Goodrich, the quiet barber known only for one distinguished act in his life, whispered into the drunk's ear, "The next time you get a shave in my shop, watch out for the razor."

The threat was delivered in a whisper and with a smile as wide as he could make it.

Some folks said the drunken cowpoke backed all the way across the barn and out the door, his hands at his neckline, and his eyes on Goodrich the barber all the time. He never told anybody what the barber had said to him and neither did the barber.

It was by this time that there had been a growing acclamation about the barber's courage and the tools that he could wield. Of course, there was to start with the saving of Mark and his mother during the bank robbery. One other story making the

44

rounds of Bullfront said Goodrich had been practicing with both pistol and rifle out on the grass and up in one of the nearby canyons. The word grew that he was getting pretty good at shooting. Along with his supposed expertise with the weapons, a growing collection of admonishments on his part, all in whispers to minor and significant threats to either Maggie or himself, began to surface in Bullfront, making him in a puzzling way a feared man no one should antagonize or mess with.

And the word was "Stay away from the widow Collins. She's spoke for." Or, "He's the only barber in Bullfront."

The wedding was planned and was only a week away, when the second robbery took place at the Bullfront Bank, with hostages taken, the town grabbing up arms, and the sheriff and deputies out on a posse chase. One robber, his horse shot out from under him as he tried to escape from town, barreled into the small house of Maggie Collins, Maggie alone in the house making her gown, Mark being taken care of by an older woman.

The robber brought her to the porch and yelled out to a gathering crowd, "Get a couple of horses up here for me, all saddled, or I kill her." His pistol was set against Maggie's head. "We're going in to get something to eat now. When I come out and you ain't got two horses here, I'll kill the lady. And you better bring me some ammunition for my Colts." He held his hand guns in the air. "Make it two boxes full."

He jammed the gun against her jaw. "She won't be pretty much longer."

"Clark," Maggie screamed. It was the only thing she said.

Clark Goodrich, barber of Bullfront, at the edge of the crowd, heard the scream.

His time, he knew, had come. All the dreams came upon him in an instant, all the dreams of becoming what he was not ... a hero despite his saving Mark and his friend on one odd chance event. He remembered how she felt in his arms at the dance. It was Elysian. Utopian. Heaven itself. Losing such a gift would be the greatest loss he'd ever know. Life would be meaningless if he lost her.

He did not know what to do, but there came a surge up through his body that he had never felt before. No idle threats, whispered in someone's ear, could save him now. No sworn use of a sharp razor could swing its edge for him now. No neckline could be threatened in this instance.

He realized one thing; Maggie was worth his life no matter what was left of his time, no matter how he might leave this new paradise; she was worth it all.

He didn't measure any actions or subsequent pains. He just moved into action.

With a quick move, he snatched a pistol from the holster of a man standing beside him. In hurried steps he was at the rail of the saloon where horses were tied to the rail. Loosening the reins of one horse, he leaped into the saddle. He spun the horse around and headed right at the crowd, which scrambled to get out of his way. And the barber of Bullfront raced the horse, a big black stallion, directly at Maggie Collins' little house at the edge of town.

The horse, driven hard by Goodrich, pounded toward the house and only drew up short as his hoofs pounded on the wooden porch. With that sudden stop the barber was tossed directly over the stallion's head and went right through the window. He landed on the floor of the front room, conscious but groggy, the pistol still in his hand, looking wildly about for Maggie.

The robber jumped into the room, saw Goodrich on the floor taking aim at him. The robber aimed his own weapon as the barber's shot went wild, hitting the wall harmlessly beside him. But a shot from behind, from a smoking pistol in Maggie's hand, killed the robber on the spot before he could pull the trigger.

"I love you, Clark," she said as she hugged him, "and, please," she added, "never tell anybody I killed a man. That's for the man of the house."

Widow Maggie Collins was kissing the barber Clark Goodrich, her hands empty, when three townsmen burst in the front door, afraid of finding the worst of the situation.

Texas Town

The times were good for just about all the people in Texas Town, though Sheriff Doug Tollivan and his deputy were constantly on their toes. Generally, there were no whispers in town. Perhaps deep and personal secrets were whispered, but everything else was said straight out and loud, like a man standing upright in his stirrups.

And the sheriff was aware that two opposing factions would be in town at the same time and knew that not one man in either the Box-Y crew or the Double Zees was apt to duck the slightest soiled word tossed about in the two saloons. The one thing Tollivan did know was they'd not start anything in the street, the store or any place of business other than one of the two saloons, The Crystal Nugget and The Twisted Saddle. The citizens, too, knew the code of the drovers; public places are out of bounds for such actions, but a saloon is often like Hell come warmed over and ready for the ultimate fire.

Texas Town, like many cow towns, came alive before a drive started as the drovers beefed themselves up for the long haul, and after a return from a successful drive to celebrate, to burn off the trail dust, to see family and old friends or new friends, or spend some money.

The last was most usual.

Tollivan also knew for a certainty that a third faction might instigate trouble for some purpose; he'd seen it before, and from usually unsuspected quarters. It was like the time that soft, mind-my-own-business Busy Boddey had fired back at tormentors, tired at last of being the dumb one in a match. He'd simply taken aim and shot brute Hardy Ackerson off his front porch as Ackerson was pounding at the door. It was one of the rare incidents as was seen in the episode now called "The Prompter's Issue." He was a stranger, not seen in the saloon before, never seen in the town before, and when two cowpokes were in a mild argument, the stranger kept alluding to "real Texans settle things out in the street, man to man."

He exhorted them in his way: "Real Texans know their way around an argument; there ain't none but face to face and out in the street. That's Texas men's home town, out in the street!"

His voice had gone up an octave or too, coming into the argument like a third knife, and before you knew it they were out

47

in the street and drawing their weapons and shooting and one man dead as ever.

But it wasn't over: when folks looked about for "The Prompter" he was nowhere in sight, and his horse was gone too. Things seemed to quiet down until a rider came into town and said he had seen an old pal riding past him in a hurry down the southern trail as he was coming up from a water hole. "Hell, I ain't seen him in five or so years, from when we rode for Slim Callahan over at Moseby's spread. He's a cousin to Zaron Zount of the Double Zees.

They warmed Hell over again those next few days until Zount was knocked off his horse on his own spread by a lucky shot from who-knows-where, and everything came to a standstill when he finally stood up, still alive, but all folks aware that death could come into their ranks in seconds and had almost taken one of the top dogs.

The sheriff went to sleep thinking of the past incidents and all the possibilities, and was deep in a post-midnight and well-earned sleep, when the sound of a shot brought him straight up in the measly cot pushed against his desk. And it was definitely a rifle shot; that meant long-range, out of sight, bushwhack kind of temerity in a town generally considered as a cowboy town where nobody was ever shot in the back … supposedly.

On rising, booting up, all he said was, "I knew it was bound to start like this."

He had no idea how accurate his assessment was, but had his rifle in hand in seconds, hat on his head, door latch in the other hand … when a second shot sounded. It was a reply shot, a defensive shot, he gauged, because it came from the opposite end of town. From near the livery came that second shot, and the first shot had come from near Betty Kline's Dress Shop at the main trail road as it left town, heading west toward Puma Hill and the mountains.

One position was secluded, he assumed, recollecting the close quarters of the building in the immediate area, and the second shot, the defensive reply, was from more open ground, and obviously at a target with background light from the newspaper where *The Texas Lookout* editor, Calvin Kyle Dupont, was laying up his next issue. The newspaper's night light was the only one that was ever lit after midnight. The big spread owners had insisted the saloons close down at midnight, agreeing that they wanted cowpokes as sober as possible saddling up for them come daybreak. They had the weight to make such a demand.

Tollivan hoped that at least one deputy heard a shot; he liked having people to talk to in the early morning, in the haze of the false dawn, in the grayness through which night stamped questions all over the day that was facing him and all folks rising to face them.

An old ache, like a twisted muscle, came anew in his neck. He had known it before, like a badge being worn, the pin sticking him, blood and consequences being drawn. "Tomorrow," it said. "Tomorrow."

He scrambled to get close to the livery, to find out if anyone was hurt, but there was nobody there; no dead man who fired back at a bushwhacker before he died, no shooter taking care of his side arm, no witness to an attempted bushwhack killing.

Big Hugh Lavery, livery owner, a noted deep sleeper, stumbled from his bed in back of the livery. He was half dressed, in one boot, holding the other boot, limping, suspenders on top of his long-john top, and sleep like pie dough hanging at his eyes. "I had a dream, Doug," he said to the sheriff, "and I swear I heard some shots."

"You heard 'em, Hughie. I heard 'em at my office. Did you see anybody? Hear anybody running down past the barn? A shot came from down this way."

"Nothing, Doug, I swear it. When I go off, I go off."

"Well, I'm going to the other end of town. But you look around and see if you find anything new or out of the ordinary around the livery. One shot came from up there and I have to check it out. I'll be back later. Send for me if you find anything." He paused and offered a suggestion to Lavery, "Put your other boot on, Hughie, before you stub your toe."

"I already done that," replied Lavery. "That got me awake." And while he bent to boot his other foot, he said, "Somethin' else I dreamed, Doug, but I can't remember what it was."

"You better check the stalls. You know how many times you said someone walked off with his horse in the night and didn't pay up."

Lavery, up for the rest of the night, slipped on his shirt, flipped red suspenders over his shoulders, and nodded at the sheriff; day had started and he might as well get going.

49

At the other end of town, *The Texas Lookout* editor, Calvin Kyle Dupont, was already questioning some folks about what and when they heard a gunshot or two gunshots. He'd gotten nothing but mumbles and figured somebody in the mix was holding back because of an allegiance one way or another. He saw the sheriff coming and figured he'd better tell him what he had garnered; not what was evidence, but a feeling still coming on him. It was evident that the sheriff couldn't do his job on such feelings, and he couldn't run a newspaper that way either.

"Cal," Tollivan said, "I kind of thought you'd be up early. You must have heard the shots last night."

"I did, Doug, but I didn't see a thing. Came right out and only heard a horse riding off, out at the fork in the road and fast, but I couldn't tell which way." He looked at the gray dawn still in its approach over Texas Town. "I don't think anybody would have seen anything, but there's an awful odd feeling hanging in the air."

The sheriff understood right away. "You figure like I do that we have opposing forces at work but doing it on the dirty side. This was bushwhacking all the way. Coward's way, Cal. Name me one of the cowpokes for either spread that'd stoop to this."

"Not one of them comes to mind," Dupont said. "Not one man I'd pin this on with my wildest guess. They're not the type."

"Meaning you think it was a stranger?" Tollivan was staring at the newspaper editor with a hard eye that also was saying something else. His words hung in the air and seemed to tip themselves in one direction.

Dupont jumped at that point. "A woman, you think?" he replied, shaking his head. His gaze went looking at the far peaks the sun was bouncing off at last, and said, "Or a strange woman at that?"

His smile was a wider-than-ever smile. "I could get a serial going on something like that." The smile came still wider. Turning saloon talk on its ear was a definite possibility.

"We could go on guessing forever," Tollivan owned up, "unless someone breaks down on a late Saturday night in The Crystal Nugget or The Twisted Saddle, with his mouth jumping like a clothesline full of duds in the wind."

Both the sheriff and the newspaper editor were nodding in agreement when Hugh Lavery came pounding up the street on a paint, his arms waving as he came on.

50

"Hey, Doug," Lavery yelled, "I remember what I forgot." He lumbered off his horse, a paint so pretty that Lavery undignified it and was unaware of the difference.

"Listen," he said. "One horse was missing from the stalls. I heard two horses riding off, toward the valley. And," he punctuated it with a full breath and a puff of his chest and a twist of his head, "I smelt perfume. A woman's perfume. I ain't smelt that kind of stuff in a dozen years."

His eyes rolled in a kind of contemplation of a new measurement or an old loss, and Dupont thought Lavery was the saddest story that he'd never get to write. And the sheriff couldn't picture Lavery behind bars, but everybody has some kind of secret he holds tight to himself ... or along with a sympathetic sheriff.

Tollivan thought, "Secrets hold a town together, and sure carve out lines of division."

"Let's go check that out, Hughie. Show me what and where, if you can."

The essence of perfume, of course, was long gone from the livery and the stall where the missing horse was stolen revealed nothing. But a search of tracks in the turn of the road out of town showed Tollivan that one of the horses was without a rider. "I think the missing horse was led off by the woman wearing the perfume."

The pause in his words was relevant. "Whoever she is, she wanted to dump suspicion on somebody else." He turned to Lavery and asked, "Whose horse was it that she took, Hughie?"

"I haven't seen him in three days. Paid for a week's rent and good care. Name's Oscar Greglin. Said he'd been working out of Puma Hill for almost a year. For Worries Williams and that neat wife of his who's a real beauty and half his age."

The Sheriff of Texas Town reached into his pocket and pinned a badge on Hughie Lavery, owner of the livery. "Hughie, you're now on the payroll and we're going to Puma Hill. Just you and me."

"We gonna see her, Doug? Ask questions?" Lavery was beaming with anticipation.

"We're gonna see him, Hughie, her husband, if we don't get to her." His voice was slightly exaggerated, but convincing.

Puma Hill sat on a slight mound at the edge of a long-running foothill in the Llano Basin. It was familiar country to

51

Tollivan, having been in Puma Hill on several posses in his early days. He didn't expect much of a change in it.

Worries Williams was a good looking gent of about 60 years, with deep eyes and a full head of hair that must have gone white before its time, for it was snow-white and had settled on him as part of his character. He wore it long, over the ears and down the back of his neck where it nestled on his shirt collar. The picture on his mantle was a starling beauty of a woman, around 30 or so years.

Williams had invited them in when Tollivan said he had some questions about one of his ranch hands.

"C'mon in, Sheriff, but I can guess it's about Oscar Greglin. He's been trouble the last month or so after a pretty good start here. I think he's finally gone off. I haven't seen him in a close to a week."

He took a deep breath and said, "You got some questions on him? Am I right about this?"

He looked at Tollivan who nodded at him and looked again at the picture of the woman on the mantle.

Williams said, "That's my wife Charity who's not here right now. She goes off every once in a while to see her sister at Gloucester Ridge. I don't get up there very often by choice, but send one of the boys with her for company coming and going. She's due in today. Greglin made the trip once. She's never had trouble at all up and back. I try to give each hand a trip. Her sister has three kids and we don't have any, so it's a real party for her when she visits. Me and her sister's husband don't see much to agree on."

Tollivan, almost locked into the beauty of the woman, managed to say, "Any recent troubles with Greglin?"

"Not really," Williams said. "One of the hands told me he said if anything ever happened to me he'd up and marry my wife and run the ranch. Can't blame a man for saying that, long as he doesn't do anything about it. Oh, I know it's been said before or thought of, but that's something comes of long drives with the cows or lonely night watching. Makes a man dream a lot. Keeps some of them going."

"You owe him any wages?"

Williams said, "I figure about a week, but he's got to show to get it, and a man that's jumped the job don't deserve full pay, I don't care what anyone says."

52

Hoof beats broke up the discussion as Williams said, "That's probably her now."

Charity Williams walked into the house and her beauty stunned Tollivan; he looked at the picture on the mantle and then back at her, and she was more beautiful than her picture. He turned red as Worries Williams said, "Sheriff Tollivan has been asking some questions of Oscar Greglin."

His wife turned red, the blush filling her cheeks. She hugged her husband and said, "Well, I didn't want to tell you, but he's been acting up. Said half a dozen times he'd marry me in a hurry if anything happened to you. I couldn't stand that, but he kept saying it every time I turned around."

She looked redder, then looked away before she said, "I took some matters into my own hands."

It all hit Tollivan in a hurry: the scent of perfume, the missing horse, the first shot in the night, the second shot, the disappearance of Greglin.

He simply said to Charity Williams, "You manage to scare him off, Ma'am?"

"Yes, I did. I scared him off and ran his horse off so he couldn't rush out of Texas Town unless he stole a horse."

Before Williams could say anything, Tollivan said, "I appreciate that, Ma'am. I know he left town by some other means. I don't have a single idea of when he'll come back ... if he ever does."

Her smile was as good as a posse running a wanted man to ground, and Worries Williams did not have as many worries as he might have imagined.

Tollivan knew how lucky Williams was. And Texas Town was probably rid of another headache of the very private kind, the whispered kind that causes worries, random gun shots without murderous intent, and character revelation, including his own.

The Black

Judd Handley had crawled through a cave, a mass of tumbled rocks, in between two sheer faces of stone, to come out on a ledge overlooking a large green expanse of mountain grass. He had never heard of any place like this in the range. No one he knew had ever mentioned a word about it. It was like a piece of heaven. Peaks of the Teton Range leaned against the sky as he looked up, only to have a black moving mass catch his eye down below at an edge of the green spread.

Handley wiped the sweat out of his eyes and took another look. The black mass was a magnificent black stallion pawing the ground, looking like a fighter who had just won a hard battle. A dozen or so mares were content down there on the rich grass. The great horse stood on his hind legs, raised his forelegs as if in a fight, or with a similar statement, then whirled about and left through a break in the far wall of the mountain. That chosen route had to come out in Reiser's Valley. Handley was sure of that; he'd find the way in from that side.

The stretch through the heart of the mountain had put a strain on his body, and it was apparent to him, as if he could feel the bruises making fast on his muscles, his skin alert to inner changes, all of it the way hard work digs deep, does one well. He did not feel badly, though. It was one way of coming out a winner in a new venture ... besides the excitement. The back of one hand was deeply bruised from a rock that had fallen on it in the cave, and he accepted it as a memento of what he was in the midst of, not what he had done already. That was a ways off he told himself.

The horse would be a prize in itself.

The animal bolted in his mind like a shot of energy. The privilege was coming alive, he could feel. To own such an animal, to train him, would make him the man he always wanted to be. This was his test, to end the endless dreaming of doing something big, of being somebody that Leeman's Fork knew.

An argument leaped inside Handley. "I've got to set a name on him, bring it to a confirmation, make it attractive, come back and catch him, this ... this ...." He stumbled and fumbled for words and simply said, "The Black." There, it was name enough, and he confirmed it in his mind. "The Black will be mine. The Black. The Black." It sat on his tongue like a spark had settled in comfortable spittle.

He kept saying the name to himself as he went back through the crevices, the sheer walls, the cave, keeping in mind the way The Black had left the valley, on the far side. And his mind set that possible route, the way in.

All the way back to Leeman's Fork, the grip of the saloon wrapping him up in its cape, he hoped he could contain himself. The Black was a superb looking animal. The mountain pasture was a prize too. He had to keep his mouth shut about the horse and the pasture. Keep all of it quiet, or else there'd be a parade of cowpokes trying to get an edge on him, a leg up.

He laughed at that last image, seeing some cowpoke get thrown by The Black as soon as he tried to sit him.

Pinky Bushwick, the bartender at The Three Rocks Saloon in Leeman's Fork, poured a beer as soon as Handley walked in the door, the sweat pouring off him, dirt and grime on his duds as if he had been thrown from his mount and needed a drink and not a doctor.

"I don't think you feel as bad as you look, Judd. You're all messed up for sure, but the look in your eyes says you got the bull by the tail. Is that a fact, or am I seeing it all wrong?"

"No, it's really nothing, Pinky. Just feel good today, not according to how I look."

"You can't tell lies with them eyes, Judd. Don't try to fool an old barkeep like me. Don't tell me you got nothing new on your mind, Judd. I've known you too long. Also, I know you ain't bound to keep a secret for too long, 'specially if it's a good one, so I'll just wait all day if I have to until you spring it." He leveled a stare from the ages as he looked over the rim of his glasses. "I swear I won't tell a soul in here."

Handley knew, of course, that promise didn't cover anyplace "outside" The Three Rocks Saloon. He gave Bushwick a smile, finished his beer and said, as he swung the door open, "I'm going to catch up some sleep, Pinky."

Both of them knew it was a lie.

Bushwick, being a bartender, a dispenser of good and not so good stuff, according what kind of money was in the exchange, had a serious hold on some of the regular customers. A few of them were the best of ferrets, and were so rewarded in their turns at the bar.

Bill Ferry, by luck or providence, was the next customer, and before he got to the bar, a shot and a beer were whipped up by Bushwick, who made as if he was sweeping coins off the bar.

Ferry smiled inwardly, knowing what was coming, but he hadn't minded any "errands" to date that Bushwick had requested, with a good hand on the tap.

Bushwick's scraper stick slid smoothly across the top the beer, sweeping excess foam from the rim. His smile was direct and forward, his eye glasses tipped like a professor's, as he assayed his new customer.

"Judd Handley," he said to Ferry, almost in a whisper, "just left here. Find out what he's up to. Where he goes in town. What he buys, if he does buy anything. Check the livery too, but make like you're just passing by. Dobrick will talk to anybody if the boss isn't around, just to kill time. See what he says."

"Gotcha," Ferry said, as he downed the shot and spent not much more time on the beer. There'd be more coming, if things worked out right for him.

Toward evening, shadows already in places, mountain peaks turning the color of the sky they slipped into, the sound of moving air coming in a new tone with a cooler message, owls on the lookout as well as bats, Ferry sauntered back into The Three Rocks Saloon. He nodded at Bushwick at the far end of the bar talking to one of the ladies from upstairs.

Bushwick dismissed the woman and a shot and a beer were on the bar when Ferry settled his elbows on the rail. "What'd you see?" Bushwick said. "What'd he do? Where'd he go? What'd he take with him?"

Ferry was full of smiles as he drank off the shot and offered a great big smile over the top of the beer mug. "You're damned right about him, Pinky. How'd you know all that? He's up to something. Loaded up at the store with vittles and such, got a new canteen, and then hired a pack mule from the livery. I followed him as far as the entrance to Reiser's Valley. I wouldn't go in there 'cause he'd see me for sure. I knowed you wouldn't want that."

"What the hell does that look like?" Bushwick said, and slipped another beer on to the counter. Again he faked the coin collection from the bar top, his eye looking for his boss sitting at a table with a few friends, in deep conversation. He wondered what that was about also, his every day waiting for answers to riddles, questions, guesses, waiting for the real wonder to happen, shake him loose from someone else's bar.

"I'm taking a day off this week. Want to go with me and have a peek when I pick a day?"

56

"Wouldn't miss it on a bet, Pinky," Ferry said, as he pushed his glass across the counter for a refill, trying to hide his smile.

The pair of rumor sleuths, wonderers, short-change specialists on life in general, were more than half a day in Reiser's Valley, when Bushwick said, "Where the hell has he gone to, Bill? You see any tracks?"

"There's lots of tracks, Pinky, a whole mess of them like wild horses been up in here. I can't follow Handley's tracks any more. They just get lost in the mix. Only thing I'm sure of is they all seem to end up at that side of the valley, over there where the wall's more than 300 feet straight up. I can't figure that out."

"Let's take a closer look over there," Bushwick said. "He's got to go someplace in here."

Judd Handley, meanwhile, had blocked up the way in and out of the secret valley by setting up limbs and brush and a few logs he had pulled in place. He was not about to let The Black get out behind him. The Black, at that time, was across the prim valley with his harem of mares, the sun coming straight down into the valley as they frolicked in the shade of a few trees.

Standing on a small ledge he had climbed from a rocky backside, he kept his eye on the stallion, thinking all the while about riding that great animal right down through Leeman's Fork main street. It would be the show of shows.

Already that morning, after setting up the blockade and setting up camp the night before, he had tried three times to throw a rope over The Black, who was an elusive target, but could not get out of the haven valley. The closest Handley got to the stallion was in a mix with a palomino mare who seemed to be the golden lass of the harem.

Handley, after several attempts, drove the palomino in behind a blow-down in a far corner of the valley and managed to erect another barrier. The Black nosed around the barrier a lot and Handley thought that would prove to be his best chance to rope him.

He was hoping he could corner The Black, whose attention might be elsewhere, with one good swing of his lasso.

While he was busily trying to make things happen, Bill Ferry, on the other side of the blocked entrance, announced his discovery to Bushwick, "Hey, Pinky, look what I found over here. I guess this means I'll be drinking free forever, huh?"

He pointed in between two huge slabs of stone that had slid saucer-like off a cliff face and had formed an archway of sorts

57

in behind another great slab of stone. "I'll bet Handley's got this place blocked off so no one will follow him in there. Let's get at it and get the way clear." He was off his mount and pulling at the pile of brush and limbs.

Bushwick, looking at the piled material, the logs on the ground, and the limbs set like rails of a fence, said, "Or he doesn't want anything to get out of there. And I bet it's wild horses or a whole herd of cows. Can't be anything else. We better not break it all down. Tie off our horses here, bring the rifles, and we'll take a peek from the other side."

He slid easily off his saddle, but with a bit of excitement showing in his face. "I knew that boy was up to something. I sure did." He swung his rifle out of the scabbard on his saddle.

Down from the ledge where he had been studying the stallion, Handley mounted his horse, swung his lasso into its working loop and started to swing it as his horse made for The Black still cavorting around the palomino mare behind the brush barrier. When The Black spun about, the lasso's whir in the air alarming him as much as the tromp of hooves, he stood defiantly on his hind legs, and the loop of the lasso settled over his neck. Handley ran his horse around a tree and the rope was secured quickly. The Black was caught, made weird noises, and reared in the air a dozen times, but the rope, choking him as he fought it, finally brought him to a standstill.

Bushwick and Ferry were yelling at that moment, saying they had a part in it all. "We want that horse, Judd," Bushwick yelled out. "You can have them other horses."

"You got it the wrong way, Pinky," Handley said, "The Black is mine. I named him before this. I tracked him in here. You can have the horses. All I want is him."

Bushwick, with the rifle in his hand, fired a shot at Handley, who returned fire immediately, a round coming very close to Ferry, who threw his rifle on the ground and said, "I don't care how many free drinks you give me, Pinky, I ain't fighting him for no horse that's his to begin with." He put his hands in the air.

Thinking better of fighting, Bushwick said, "Can we have them horses?"

"They're all yours, Pinky. I want The Black and he stays here with me until I break him or he breaks me." He finished off by saying, "And you boys better keep quiet about this place or the

58

sheriff and the owner of the saloon ain't going to like what I tell them."

Bushwick and Ferry planned how they'd drive the mares back to town, and set about getting it done. In a matter of hours they were out of the valley and headed back to town, after rebuilding the barrier at Handley's direction.

"Just in case," as Handley explained it.

Four days after he left town, Judd Handley rode into town sitting one of the finest looking stallions anybody in town had ever seen, including the livery men and all the old timers living in Leeman's Fork.

Bushwick and Ferry has already spread the word about how they had helped young Judd Handley catch the great stallion in a daring escapade in a secret valley they were sworn not to talk about.

The Circus in the Valley of Ten Chiefs

Kiel McQueen, extraordinary horse rider, was in love …
with the circus, with the Wild West, and mostly with Mary
Maguire, the best of all equestrian riders, and the most beautiful
woman he had ever seen. But he hated the constant work they had
to do to keep the circus going, even though better days were
ahead. Circus owner Oscar Parmenter often said, trying to raise
hopes of his crew, "We'll most likely be riding on the railroad for
our next trip." The year was 1879 and they were bound for the
Valley of Ten Chiefs, and the bustling town of Caliber, in the
Wyoming territory, on the same rough roads of travel. The name
of the valley, though, excited McQueen and brought up all the
images he had heard or read about life in the west full of robbers
and road agents, and Indians in great encounters. His sack held a
few copies of stories about Wild Bill Hickok and Kit Carson, each
of them read nearly clean through the printer's ink, and a hand-
written copy of Ned Buntline's play titled "Scouts of the Prairie"
that a bartender in Chicago had given to him.

No circus had ever been set up in the Valley of Ten Chiefs
until Parmenter had taken care of all arrangements with the town
council of Caliber by telegraph. The commitment was to help
celebrate the Grand Reunion of the Great Posse Chase, and the
25th year of that supposed noble undertaking. Unknown to
Parmenter, an entrepreneur of the first order, some of those riders
were still hanging around, though a bit long in the tooth and slow
on the draw.

What Parmenter did not like were surprises that might
seriously reduce circus profits. He'd be wary in a new locale.

But surprises were coming from the Great Posse Chase
itself, on both sides of the memorable event.

The family of the two men hunted and hung in the chase
had never agreed with the court verdict of guilty, claiming the
judge was involved in a personal issue, which could have come
to light on the day of his death from a self-inflicted wound. The
drummer who found the body said the judge had a note grasped
in his hand. The drummer hastened into town to tell authorities
what he had discovered.

The note, however, was never revealed by the two deputies
who brought the judge's body back from the wide grass of the
valley. Both deputies, as it turned out, were related to the judge,
nephews who had grown up under his care.

The whole message of the great posse chase went legendary, carrying, of course, different tunes from the different sides. Unrest was attached inevitably to the background of the posse.

Other than that page of Caliber's history, the first thing that went wrong for Parmenter in the whole escapade happened when a direction sign was moved on the trail to the valley. That move sent the string of circus wagons on the wrong path for a good part of a day. A mountain man, on first sight thought to be a grizzly bear, packed in heavy clothes and fur, set them straight for a small trade of furs for food and supplies.

"Do me the privilege of a trade for some food and ammunition," he had said, "and I'll give you these furs and set you on the right course for Caliber, 'cause you're a might off the way you're headin'."

Parmenter, without the slightest doubt, figured the mountain man, from a description provided by some of the circus riders who had seen him earlier, moved the trail marker in the first place, and ambled along, nearby but unseen, until he could benefit by a providing correct directions.

Parmenter told everybody in the troupe that he wished he could send a new posse after the mountain man, "but they'd be out there for weeks tracking down a man who doesn't want to be found."

"That," said McQueen, "sure sounds a lot like the Great Posse Chase we're going to celebrate. Doesn't that sound like a whole hatful of irony for you?" Prior to this discussion, McQueen had been nursing the deep thought that this show was going to be different from all the others. He did not know where that thought had originated, but it was there, moving toward the surface.

Parmenter shrugged off McQueen's comment. He was expecting a good crowd, a good exchange of money, a bit of gold in the mix, and too, a bit of skullduggery tossed in as usual. The circus, no matter where it went, woke up people en route by setting up, providing new excitement while it ran, and nearly as much when it packed up to move on. The fancy riders, like Mary Maguire and Kiel McQueen, were his main attractions, for the whole west moved by horse, in the saddle or being hauled in a wagon or cart, though changes were fully on the way.

Parmenter looked at the resources of an area before agreeing to bring the circus to a town. A few good-sized ranches were in the area of the Valley of Ten Chiefs, and at least a dozen mines, prosperous ones, were actively worked in the hills. Also, who knew how many mountain men lived in the high areas around the valley who'd come to the circus, anxious for news and noise for as long as they could stand it? Plus, there was the whole town of Caliber ready to focus its attention on his performers and other attractions that were the backbone of any circus.

At the previous location where the show had drawn a sizeable throng, Parmenter kept up his tirade on moving day to get all the equipment broken down and onto the wagons for the next push. "Get it all packed up, boys, for we have a great site this time out, in the Valley of Ten Chiefs in Wyoming where we'll be part of a great celebration, the 25th anniversary of the Great Posse Ride."

He realized he'd have to put some butter on the other side of the bread for the crew, and laid it on. "It promises to be an eye-opening and memorable event. The people will be coming from all over the territory to join the celebration and see us perform. I can't wait for all of us to get there and make a good show for them."

Kiel McQueen, said, "Hey, Oscar, I hope none of those chiefs are still hanging around looking for scalps, and The Great Posse Ride has got hung the bad dudes they were after." The words were part of the feeling growing inside him, the edginess coming nearer to light.

He forced a chuckle as he looked around at the other riders and handlers and exhibitionists of various disciplines. "Along with itinerant help, we're working at what we pulled down only two weeks ago and set out for this place. Now, we're ready to leave again. The cycle's endless and monotonous. It requires too much work for skilled people. I know we receive lots of fanfare from every audience that watches our fancy riding acts, but the roads we travel and the trails we fight with nothing but plain labor don't get matched by the receptions we get. We ought to get a bigger piece of the pie, is all I'm saying while I have the chance."

He dropped the roll of canvas he was hoisting to the back of a wagon. "You know, Oscar," he continued, "there are places back east that bring better crowds. We ought to think about heading back there sometime. You have to admit the routes out here go practically from nowhere to nowhere."

He was looking at the heart of the circus, his fellow fancy riders; they were the best around, artists of equestrian entertainment the west was starved for. There were also trapeze acts and acrobats with beautiful women, gangs of clowns, tightrope walkers, and the brass band with horn and drum tooters. He could hear the wild animals of the circus menagerie, some roaring at continued confinement or discomfort in their cages, but they were unique attractions for youngsters who'd otherwise never see African lions or tigers from India or huge elephants standing on their hind legs at the mere sound of a whistle.

McQueen had been in a couple of troupes before this one, always looking for the permanent place where he could rest on his laurels and not have to fight the hard ways of traveling the west. "I keep hearing you say the railroad will be the new route for us on the next trip, all comfy and easy aboard a train. We'd even have a special car for meals and not be slowed to 10 or 15 miles a day on the worst roads that can be found. That does sound pretty good."

McQueen's eyes spotted Mary Maguire in the midst of listeners. She was the best female equestrian artist he had ever seen and he was totally in love with her. It was the reason he hung around this circus, but she was the niece of Parmenter, which put a hitch in his hopes. She was a special lady who could ride like the wind while standing on her horse, and with her outfit helped catch the eye of every man watching the show. When she did her pyramid act, up on the shoulders of two men on paired horses, the applause was uproariously loud. At every skilled spot she drew a huge ovation, clapping and whistling abounding the whole time. And young men hung around at all hours to get extra looks at her, see her off the horse, to see how she shaped up otherwise.

He'd have to keep his eye on her all the time they were in the Valley of Ten Chiefs, and in Caliber itself.

That afternoon, from an opening in the foothills, they finally saw the rooftops of Caliber sitting on the edge of the grass a few miles off and a clear road for the rest of the way.

Caliber sat up and paid attention as the circus came to town.

As the displays and booths were being set up out in the valley, a short walk from town, McQueen became aware of the first physical concern about the show this time around. At the edge of the small crowd watching the crew go about their tasks, he noticed an old timer, the kind he'd seen before with the hard eyes calling down the years, looking at him, as though he was being sized up.

McQueen thought, "He's not looking at me because he's trying to see what a good rider does in his spare time. This dude

63

doesn't even know me, or what I do. Why not check him instead, hail him out?"

As though he was just passing by, he neared the old man, and their eyes locked.

"I'm one a them," the old man said. "One of the posse riders you folks are all celebratin'. I guess you knowed that way you was lookin' at me."

"How many of you are left?" McQueen said. "But I saw you looking at me."

"You get right to it, don't cha? Almost like you know what I'm gonna say. I like that in a young feller. And it sure is a mystery to me." His eyes blinked like he was sifting through the years looking for a specific image. "You know one of us dies every five years."

He paused, rolled his eyes again in his count, and added, "And on this same day, like it was writ on the calendar. This same day every five years, like we was all to fault for doin' what we were told to do, go get the killers. But they're gettin' us, only slower at it. Don't cha call that a mystery, Mr. Circus Man?"

"I'm Kiel McQueen; I'm a fancy rider in the show. What's your name?"

The old man with the hard eyes put out his hand and said, "I'm Luke Kingsbury and I ain't throwed a leg up on a horse in a year or more. Gets me right back here," and his right hand passed around his waist and clamped on his near backside. "Right about there, like maybe where the bullet that's comin' to me in my turn might find itself, causin' the same kinda pain."

He paused again in his counting and said, "Today bein' the day." Over his shoulder he looked. "Don't nobody ever see anybody, though, except the dead one is one of the riders in the posse. Every last one a them killed on this day, the same day it all ended for them two fellers on the only tree you could see in them rocks up there." He nodded off to the great mountain to the west, a mean looking mountain that McQueen hoped he'd never have to pass through or over.

"Do you know who's doing the killing? Have any ideas?" McQueen could not take his eyes off the old man's face, where he could nearly count the years by the wrinkles.

"I'm thinkin' they're relatives of those two that got killed after two weeks of chasin' through the mountains, them like the ghosts they was." And he stopped, thought it over, and spoke again, in the same tone of voice, "Real ghosts. We'd see 'em and

64

then they was gone. For two weeks it was, like us bein' pulled into a pit fight with a mad pit dog who wasn't showin' himself until dark when it wouldn't count no how."

"You saw both of them die up there?" He tossed his head toward the mountains.

McQueen's question seemed too cautious for Kingsbury. "Son," he said, "I seen dyin' and I seen killin' and that was killin' all the way. We knowed that, most of us. Too much fuzzy stuff goin' on at the trial and that damn fool of a judge killin' hisself and his note never bein' showed not for one minute."

He was measuring again. "Course, all that came after them boys was killed, that bein' the day that comes back in its haunt every year." Over his shoulder he looked one more time, as though the move was set by a pocket watch. "He's probably in that crowd now, maybe lookin' right at me, who does it. I don't see no others from the ride, but there's only three of us left anyways. Tim Chambers, Miles MacDougall, and me."

A change came over him; the wrinkles and lines deepened on his face, the way the chisel wielder of history makes his marks to last until the final breath. There'd be no mistaking him anywhere for anybody else in the world; he could have said, "Luke Kingsbury, killer, about to be kilt."

It was that kind of a day.

McQueen wondered if such thoughts would hang on during his act; the awed feeling, the expectations affecting his performance. He didn't dare say, "The certainty." But it certainly ran through his mind.

The show went on in the afternoon, with plans to go until darkness cut the trick rides down, freed the tight rope walkers and the acrobats and the trapeze aerialists, and lamps and candles carried the gambling and the multiple booth games to conclusion. When McQueen made his first loop of the day around the large ring laid out on the grass, he looked for Kingsbury and did not see the old man who was marking his time. He did not see two other curious faces, also marked by age, he had lit on when talking to Kingsbury, and he did not see the sheriff or his deputy.

That revelation surprised him; sheriffs and deputies always made a point of keeping a sharp eye out for thieves, cheats, and circus hustlers working the crowd. In all towns where they had set up and run the enterprise, the local sheriff or marshal was a presence one could count on, making circuits the whole day

65

through the crowd the way one would patrol for votes in a new election.

In Caliber it was different, with no lawmen around, and was that way until darkness descended and the lamps went out at the circus booths. The stars, dim at first, came loose from their hideaways. The caged animals, under that starry clock, made different sounds in the nocturnal rhythm, and McQueen kept watch on the Maguire wagon until he fell asleep under his own wagon, Mary on his mind until there came no more thought.

In the morning, after a decent sleep, wondering why he thought of Mary and Kingsbury at the same time, the crew already mixing odd tasks with morning duties, he heard about the death of Miles MacDougall. "A rider of the old posse," said one of the crew, repeating what he had heard from a town person looking for a day's work. "They found him in the back of the livery, hanging by his neck from a beam. He was cold when they found him. Must have been hanging there all night. Even the horses was still."

"Who found him?" McQueen said as he looked around the morning gang, still looking for Kingsbury.

"The sheriff was going on an early ride and found him. Cut him down and called the coffin maker and put him to work right away. They want to put him down kind of quiet, so the whole circus won't get spoiled by a new murder on an old score."

Parmenter, on the prowl, yelled out, "You going to jaw all day or do some work? We got a bigger crowd coming today. Lots of money. Get at it."

Mary Maguire, shining like dawn worked on her complexion, sauntered by. "Good morning, Kiel. Thank you for the nightly vigil. Is it uncomfortable down there? Bad as it looks?" Her gaze drifted to the ground beneath his wagon.

"No, Mary. It was a little warm last night. Anyway, I crave the stars, the lot of them. Gives night the best look of all."

Her response kept him right on his own track. "I know exactly what you mean." Her gaze swept down the valley, past the layout of the circus, and a querulous look sat on her face. "Do you know why they call this place The Valley of Ten Chiefs? That's a strange name, and I've heard Indians, at least the ones around here, don't bury their dead but tend to burn them, like cremation."

McQueen said, "I only know what I've heard about the name from an old timer. Once there was a huge Indian powwow here and the chiefs had retired to a lodge to discuss waging war on some other tribes. There was a landslide and they were buried under tons of rock."

"I'll wager there was no war after that."

"I'd never bet against you, Mary," he replied, "no matter what was at stake."

Parmenter wasted no time in his rounds. "Come on, Mary, leave the boys alone. We've got too much to do. Big crowd coming today. I hope you slept well."

McQueen jumped in. "Hey, Oscar, did you hear about the murder last night? One of the remaining posse from the great chase was hung in the livery."

"I heard all about that nonsense. Don't pay any attention to it. Besides, Injuns aren't any of our worry." Drawing his pocket watch from his trouser pocket, he stared at it, looked at the sun, shook his head and started to walk off.

"You better hope so," Mary said, "because I do."

The circus started humming, Parmenter continued his rounds, and before long McQueen was on his last loop around the ring, his last ride of the evening, when he spotted Kingsbury in the crowd.

They met after the performances ended for the day and the lamps were lit in the booths, the crowd almost doing an about face to change their pleasures.

"Luke," McQueen said, "I looked for you all day. I thought you were gone. One of the posse killers catching hold of you. Where've you been?"

"I was hidin'," he said, "where they wouldn't find me; in the loft of the livery."

"You saw it all, didn't you? Who was it?"

"The sheriff and his deputy. Quick, no noise, rapped him one and hung him unconscious. He never knew what hit him or who."

"What are you going to do? I know the marshal over at Micah's Hat. He's straight as they come."

"I won't need him. Me and Tim Chambers got it all fixed. Them two ain't goin' to get us. There's goin' to be another landslide in the Valley of Ten Chiefs, and it ain't goin' to take another five years to get done."

"The sooner the better," McQueen said, just as Mary Maguire appeared out of the darkness.

"I hope you were talking about me," she said.

67

Before McQueen could answer, the old posse rider said, "We sure were, Miss. This Valley won't be the same once you two leave here. Trust me on that."

"I do," Mary Maguire said. "I can't wait forever. I watch him watching me every night. It's not all fair."

"Not much is these days," Kingsbury offered, "except when things get took care of."

Darkness swallowed them up forever.

The Raggedies

Sheriff Bill Dobson had an uneasy feeling that something was going on in his town, Ross Corners, on a twist of Colorado's Blue River. The country around was scenic with great views in every direction, the folks were generally nice folks who said the sheriff kept his ear close to the ground, that sooner or later he'd hear everything on the trail. But he did not have the slightest clue about this new undercurrent.

Neither did Caleb Thornwell, Jr., 11-year old son of the livery owner, sitting on a rock in a cave he'd never been in before, the newest member of "The Raggedies," a name they adopted because all of them wore hand-me-downs or "worn to the nub" clothes. He kept shaking his head, amazed at what was going on, amazed at how kids, all of them near his age, had this grasp on things, on the whole town it appeared, and kept it all in "The Book." Caleb was smaller than the others, and probably less interested than his pals, but his father, more than just him realizing it, had a handle on much of everything that went on in town, like the comings and goings of people using his livery, at least for overnight stays. Young Thornwell, without knowing it, was a political pawn, but Billy Talmon, beyond his years, knew his way around and he'd be able to use this new boy who seemed to lack for tight friends.

Thornwell didn't have a hint at what The Book was, though the other kids, these new friends of his, spoke of it with admiration, love, whatever was coming at him that he couldn't figure out. They seemed to be on fire every time they talked about it, The Book.

Suddenly, at the other end of the cave, away from the canyon entrance, a raspy sound was heard. Andy Marston, another kid from town, crawled into the cave at the back entrance, whistled twice, both times lightly, listened for a few seconds, heard someone whistle back, and said, "Is that you in there, Billy? You got The Book with you?"

The cave was in the heart of the Rockies, not far from the town of Ross Corners, sitting on the picturesque high end of the Blue River.

"Yuh, it's me, Andy, me and Benjy," Billy Talmon said, "and we got a new deputy. Caleb Thornwell from the livery. He's here with us. Course he ain't got anything new for us right now, being so new, but we'll be able to count on him down the trail."

69

Feeling like he was buttering the bread with a half-pound of butter and a load of jam, he said, "We'll sure count on Caleb helping us out here. That's one fine new recruit we got with us now. It's plain old good news in itself for The Book."

He paused with command presence, and then continued, "You got anything new, Andy? Anything to report for The Book?" He was able to stand up easily in that section of the cave. It caused him think of an Indian totem, which made him feel slightly exalted, especially for a kid almost a man in some things. The light from the flames threw his shadow on the wall and across the upper arch of the cave. He felt bigger than he actually was.

"Sure have, Billy. Wait'll I get up in there and get myself set."

He crawled almost all the way in until he saw the small fire and the silhouettes of his friends. The comfort zone grasped him; hanging loose with friends was one of his few joys. Much of his time was spent in his father's barn, mucking out, cleaning and maintaining the few possessions needing such work, and not having much time to spend with his new horse. He missed those opportunities and felt lucky with his "membership" in the gang.

Excitement ran all over him and the others could feel it even before he said, "I got something for The Book. I really got something this time." A deep breath seemed to swallow him for a few seconds. "You won't believe this."

"You said that last time, Andy," Talmon said. "You ain't got nothing yet. Wait'll you hear what Benjy saw. It could knock you right out of the saddle. It's great stuff for The Book." He was upbeat and excited, waiting to spill the goods, but knew Andy had to have his chance in the sun in the cave. He almost laughed all the way through that private interchange, but wouldn't say so to the others ... let them find out for themselves, if they could.

"So what'd you see, Andy? It's got to be right up in front of you, seeing it. Knowing who's in the mix of it like he don't ever belong there. We're not interested in who's sneaking into whose bedroom when the old man's away, or who plays around out there under that tree that's off on the trail into town. Lots of folks play there coming or going. That don't count with us. Seems like a lot of folks tend to stuff like that."

"It's Sheriff Dobson," Andy said. "He carries a stick stuck down in the rifle sheath of his saddle and he tugs it onto his own small branding iron he carries in his saddle bag and marks a cow every once in a while and just waits for him, I bet, to show up in a count on someone else's place. When they tell him, he says it wandered off from his small herd and it's kinda come back to him."

"He do it only the once?

"Nope. Not on your life. I saw him a couple of times do it. Like he looked around and made sure nobody was seeing him, too. I wanted it to be good for The book."

"Where was you?"

"In the bushes. He didn't see me."

"Where was your horse?"

"I walked out there. I was gonna do a little fishing the first time it happened, and keep my eyes out for something to put in The Book. I was thinking about what you said before, about horses giving us away any time, them and their shoes of iron. That was because I saw him kind of sneaking around, going out of town them few times, and decided to walk out there, like I was really going fishing. What the heck, it didn't bother me none."

"Did he start a fire to heat the iron up?"

"Nope, like he did before when I found him," Andy said. "He found a fire still warm from branding being done before he got there. The Rickets' crew had left it and he had been watching them. He plain rode in and put on a few sticks and heated his iron and used the stick to handle it and stuck it on a dogie, then skedaddled out of there. The dogie just walked off."

"Sounds like we got him, but we got to find that branding iron and copy it. That'll sure go in The Book, Andy. But we gotta find that iron of his. That's a good piece of information. We'll nab him when the time comes. You did good. I always thought the sheriff was on the thin side of the law. My pa says it all the time. He don't trust nobody anyway."

Andy said, like he was reporting to the commanding officer of a cavalry regiment, "Just doing my duty, Sheriff." He could have snapped off a salute, his retort was so business-like. "You gonna put that in The Book right now? Right now so's I can see it?" He was as proud as when his own colt was born and he called him Moondog, a name he had heard from an old Indian.

"Sheriff" Billy Talmon, a little taller than his friends, a bit more age showing in his face and eyes, who had "organized" The Raggedy Sheriff and His Deputies, said, "I sure am, Andy. I sure am." With a smooth and deliberate move, he slid his hand inside his shirt and slowly pulled out a slim volume measuring about 6 inches wide and 8 inches long. The cover of finished leather

71

showed a dark, roughly drawn title of reading "Our Book of Law Breakers." The slim volume was crowded with pages, and looked to be at least an inch thick.

They simply called it, reverently at any mention, "The Book." They held it to be their answer to all local problems, their witness to the wrongs they had seen, and every wrong had a witness and a name wrapped together by a date. They were meticulous entries, noted and sworn to.

Talmon opened The Book to a page not fully used and wrote a new entry: Sheriff Dobson sneak branded a Rickets' dogie. He carried a small branding iron with no long handle in his saddle bag. He carried a wood handle in his rifle pouch. He was alone. He was seen this day, as signed below here. Witness, Andy Marston, June 11, 1877." The last entry was made by Marston beaming in the face as he did so.

Talmon followed up that activity by saying, "Now I'll read what Benjy saw and what we wrote in The Book."

There followed a momentary silence as Talmon prepared to witness a prior entry. The silence was an announcement in its own right, a most solemn occasion of a lawman's deposition.

"Banker Rauthour has a stash of money outside of town under rocks in Brace Canyon. He buries it at or near dark, making sure he's alone. He collects some rocks to take back with him faking his search for silver or gold. He's done this on six different Saturday nights. I watched them all from the first time he snuck there and I was looking for my part in The Book. The money comes out of his pocket, like he brung it from someplace, and he adds it to the stash he keeps in a buried box. Witness, Benjy Smithers, June 8, 1877."

From the cave opening a whistle sounded once, and then a second time, then an answering whistle sifted through the cave like a small echo, or a heartbeat. "It's me, Henry Raymond. I'm comin' in."

A dragging noise was heard as Henry Raymond made his way toward the light. The other members could hear him puffing away, which sounded like more news coming, another page being used to "pin the tail on the donkey," as Talmon had once described their secret testimonies. "We ain't playing games," he had vouched, "but we'll sure pin the tail on the donkey when we unload The Book on the town."

"This is another good un," Henry Raymond said, sputtering about his news item of sorts. "I don't know what it means, but there's sure something going on that starts with Perkins the coffin maker."

He came to the fire, sat on a stone and looked as pleased as he was mysterious.

"Okay, Henry," Talmon said, "Let's have it. What this time?"

"We know Perkins never has a coffin ready when someone dies or gets killed and always has to make it from scratch. You know how he fusses around and makes a great commotion out of a little noise, like being important on the day he thinks is his day and not for the dead person. But when Dickson went down yesterday in that face-off with Caruthers, there was one ready, right in his shop. I saw it right inside the shop when he opened the door and the cut-up stuff and the shavings were still on the floor. And him and Doc Wentworth put Dickson's body right into it after the doc said Dickson was dead as he's ever going to be."

"Yuh, okay," Talmon said. "So what?"

"He's supposed to get buried today."

"We all know that. What else?"

"He wasn't in it this morning. He ain't in it now."

"Who isn't?"

"Dickson ain't in the coffin. Just a couple of sacks full of dirt in there. I saw it all this morning. I got right inside from the back. It's easy, like he's got nothing to protect anyway."

"Anybody see you pokin' around?"

"I'm a Raggedy Deputy, Billy. Nobody saw me. I made sure of that. That's just the stuff we practiced them times you was showing us."

Talmon was standing as tall as he imagined the totem to be, and his silhouette from the fire had leaped up the wall and onto the arched top of the cave. Then he moved his hands and arms the way he had practiced and saw the looks in their eyes and how it spread on their faces; they were awed and afraid of him and showed great respect for him. He moved his arms again the way he had studied the wings of vultures eyeing a body or carrion in a canyon or out on the grass. He could tell these kids to do anything and they'd do it.

He'd been in the cave an hour before anybody else came, retrieved some fire wood from a secret stash taken care of in advance of its need, started the fire, saw the silhouette, the ominous shadow he cast up and over everything in the cave,

73

quickly read again the power and persuasion in the whole matter, and planned his day and some days that would follow by design.

"He" was The Sheriff of the Raggedies. Nobody disputed that. And his territory was growing. Caleb Thornwell was a continuing sign of that growth. The whole schoolhouse could come under his influence, but, as he had already sifted almost every one of them through his mind, most of the rest might not be able to handle the weight of the law. Mistakes he could not afford or tolerate. Law was the uppermost in all of this: though he heard something in his mind repeating the words all the time, as if an argument might be at work. Caleb's recruitment showed for the good of the organization, and the others surely'd try to out-do themselves on their contributions just to show off a little, doubly spurred by the son of the liveryman who knew so much. That man knew at sight where horses had been ridden, how hard, what care they received, what their feed was like, what saddle sores had to say. Some folks said he even developed reasons behind the selection of a horse's name. Few knew, though, that he wished he had thought of Moondog, which young Marston had named his colt. He loved that name for a horse. His own son never thought of names like that.

In the midst of his reverie and planning ideas, Andy Marston, still excited, Billy Talmon's shadow pressing down on him, said, "Billy, when are we going to spring The Book on the town?" His mouth was wide open, his fists formed like new punctuation.

Like the others, he almost bowed as the words slipped out of his mouth. "How will we do it? We can't tell the sheriff or the town council because half of them are already in The Book. How'll we do it, Billy?"

"Oh, gosh, Billy, I can't hardly wait," yelled Benjy Smithers, standing beside Talmon, almost as tall. "How long we gonna wait, Billy. What'll some of those faces look like when they hear what we got locked up in The Book?" He clasped his hands in anticipation.

It happened in Ross Corners' Crazy Colt Saloon, at the far end of the bar but nearest the piano, where Sheriff Bill Dobson, a smiling, outward and generally pleasant fellow who'd been on the job for five years, talked quietly with a couple of townies. The sheriff looked around innocently, set a new expression on his the way most people change subjects, and said, "You gents see anything funny going on in town, like something being hid from us?"

The quizzical look on his face, authentic as could be, said he as the sheriff of the town was officially puzzled by some aspect within Ross Corners' daily business. Most of the men in the saloon would agree that he was a pretty good man on the job, kept doggedly at solving issues, keeping the peace, enforcing most of the laws enacted by the Town Council.

One of the men said, "Bill, it's funny you should ask that. I don't think much goes on in town that ever gets by you. You seem to have a handle on everything and some of it, I'd bet, is even private." He chuckled as if to make the others chuckle with him, and they did so agreeably, for each one of them had a penchant for listening to tales of other folks; it fed their curiosity.

Another of the group, Jake Welton, said, "Are you talkin' about the kids, Bill, how they head out sometimes like they're goin' fishin' and I rarely see them on the stream, even in the best spots? We all know where the best spots are. We've known them for years."

"Where do they go," Dobson said, "if they don't go fishing?" he leaned in also and lowered his voice. "That's what I was asking about. They seem awful damned busy about something. Talmon's kid, Marston's kid, Hank Raymond's kid, a few others too, and I don't know what they're up to, but it ain't fishing, like Jake says."

Welton said, "Hell, Bill, I ain't about to follow some kids out there maybe meetin' a few girls on the sly. Sometimes lookin' bad is lookin' pretty good as far as the girls are concerned. These kids ain't far away from bein' real cowboys, you know. 'Member how we fooled around even before we drove a few cows for our own folks?" He made them all laugh when he said, "Damn, but I wish I knowed then what I know now."

Dobson, with the quick smile, said, "From what I heard, Jake, once you and Ellen got tussled up, it was all over for you. What's it, close on 30 years now?"

They all laughed again and Dobson walked away as if he had another call to make, an arrest to be made, a law to be enforced. He could be quizzical and businesslike in one and the same manner, and the others accepted his quick departure as immediate business of the badge.

He walked back to his office thinking he had put the bee in their bonnet. He'd let it buzz around a bit. As usual, the buzz would come back to him in some manner, in short order. It always did.

Jake Welton, on the way back to his spread down trail about four miles, dropped in to see Caleb Thornwell when he saw him working on a horse in front of the livery.

"Caleb," he said, "just sayin' hello on my way home. How's the family?" Then, as his usual manner, he jumped right into things that sat on his mind. "Bill Dobson was askin' us if we knew what the kids is up to, bein' kind of secret about somethin' he can't figure what. You got any ideas. Most of them are your boy's age, I'd guess."

"Not a thing I know, Jake, but I'll sure ask young Caleb. Get him out of the lion's mouth afore he gets snapped up."

"It'd be interestin' we get somethin' Bill don't know and drop it in his lap. Wouldn't that be a twist?" He mounted his horse and departed, saying, "You hear anythin', Caleb, let me in on it. Sure would enjoy that twist." He laughed as he rode away.

Later that evening, young Caleb walking back from his most recent "fishing" excursion, no catch evident, and quickly noticed his father sitting in front of the livery, idling away. He was not an idling man and Caleb could tell he had something on his mind, the way he was twisting his pipe in both hands, knocking it against the hitching rail and nothing falling out because there was nothing there to start with. It was a sure give-away that his father was "mind-set," a term he had used numerous times.

"Catch anything, son? Don't appear so to me, less you ate them already. You boys cook out there?"

Caleb was caught up immediately by the apparent change in attitude. His father rarely asked him where he had been, what he done, and he was not prepared for the encounter.

"Not a bite, Pa. Don't know why you folks say those are the best places, by the second creek and past the big curve in the river. Nothing at all."

The sun had disappeared behind one mountain peak, the dust had settled in the road behind him and behind the last rider passing by, horses nickered and neighed in the livery, and an ominous silence sat around his father, still tapping his empty pipe against the hitch rail, almost like the telegrapher at the station, someone somewhere knowing what those taps on the key meant.

Here, it was him.

The funny feeling persisted that "this was it." A lot in his short life was about to be undone. How much could he hold back? His father knew so much; maybe he knew all of it already. The feeling ran through him like a series of quick shivers. The scenes in the cave surrounded him as if he was sitting there on that one stone he always sat on. The smell of dead ashes came into his nostrils as sharp as the lower barn being mucked out. Booming past his ears came Billy Talmon's strong voice, much more than a mere echo; it could have been a steam engine grinding its slow-downed way into the station. Bang. Bang. Bang. Chug. Chug. Chug. Words. Words. Words.

The faces of Andy and Henry and Benjy and the others, staring at Billy, reared up in a space behind his eyes; they could have been taunting him.

"What have you and the boys been up to, Caleb? And I want no lies and no tomfoolery out of you. You just take a deep breath and break it loose for me. I'm your father and the most important one for you in all of this, whatever it is, and I hope it's nothing bad you've hitched yourself to."

There it was, out in the open, all the stuff that had been bothering him.

Caleb Thornwell, livery owner, sat in the sheriff's office with Sheriff Dobson, and three members of the town council. He figured he had made the longest speech he'd ever made in his life, knowing he had their strict and complete attention from his first words:

"The kids, a bunch of them, have a book with all kinds of stuff in it about some people; I don't know who. Maybe somebody in this room is in it. They call it 'The Book' and I hear it's loaded with enough stuff to put some folks in jail, or maybe worse. They've been collecting information for almost a year. They meet in a cave up in the mountains. They make reports on what they've seen happening and enter it right into The Book. I hope to hell I'm not in it. That Talmon kid is the ringleader." He said it like Billy Talmon was a criminal of the first order. "Makes the others report what they saw, then writes it in The Book and makes them sign it as witnesses, and they put dates on it too. It's like they're getting ready for court, only Talmon says, from what I hear, he wants to give it to the Territorial Marshall, and not give it to anybody in Ross Corners. That includes you too, Sheriff, which would make me a little uneasy if I was you."

Sheriff Dobson shivered a bit in his seat, figuring some folks in the room would hang him in a second if they'd seen what he had done on several occasions. At least, they'd send him off to prison for a good spell. Survival in a way meant keeping his mouth shut or jumping into the middle of the issue.

The badge felt heavy on his chest, a sensitive weight leaning on his heart.

He leaned in on the group. "It's not right," he said, "that kids have done this. Hell, they could have made things up to get even with older people, plain made errors all along the way." He coughed and stammered and stood up and sat down and stood up and sat down again. The sweat ran on his nose like raindrops.

"It's not their job," he exclaimed, standing up again, waving his hands. "That's me and my deputies' job. That's what we get paid for. Whatever we do, and without a lot of noise or fuss, we've got to get that book. Otherwise, it would only set things up for a whole damned vigilante movement and you know what the hell happened over in Claremont when that gang got going. It killed the town in less than a year. We can't let that happen here. This town is too pretty to let it go to pieces over some kid sheriffs playing at games."

The group talked for nearly three hours, hashing things over, developing a plan of sorts, setting a few rules they'd have to follow. None of them knew if they were in The Book or not.

At least, they did not show it outwardly. But all of them wanted to get The Book in their hands, perhaps for one hour.

Pre-dawn, the men at the evening meeting left town and staked out all the places around where the cave might be, knowing there were dozens of caves they had been in and many they had not. Before the sun jumped at Ross Corners over the rim of a mountain, the men were in various sites, each with a wide view of certain sections of the land.

They were waiting on the boys, The Raggedies. Each one realized that Caleb Thornwell had an inside edge on them.

Dobson wondered if any of them were as worried as he was. He wondered why it had to come to this, "because of a bunch of nosey kids." Then, for the first time since the issue started to unfold, he smiled and remembered his own dreams and hopes as a kid. He promised himself he'd be as tactful, and as kind, as he could be.

A sun's ray dipped inside his collar, warmed him. A stone, thrown in a high arc, glanced off a section of cliff and clinked off two other surfaces and banged on the floor of the canyon.

Bill Talmon, walking up off the trail into the mountains, looking behind him every so often, picked up another stone and flung it higher than the one first tossed. This one had the same flight and the same noises attached to it. Dobson remembered quick pieces of his life he had not thought of in years.

Talmon, Dobson noted, carried nothing in his hands. He wondered if The Book was stuffed inside his shirt or if he had not brought it along. That'd mess things up, for sure.

Looking around again, Talmon picked up another stone and flung it higher yet. The stone made louder noises as young Talmon ducked behind a rock, peering out occasionally.

"That's one damned smart kid," Dobson said to himself as he watched Talmon scan the entire area for anyone who might have followed him.

Satisfied he was not followed, he scaled a section of wall, slipped into a fissure, appeared again at another break, the way one passes behind a large window, and disappeared for good.

"Ah," Dobson said, "there's the cave of The Raggedies." He puffed with admiration of the boy, though his feelings were all fighting with each other. "I best forget that thought," he said to himself. "I'll just wait to see who else shows up."

From a jumble of rocks he saw a second boy squeezing his way through another fall of rocks that had lain in place for maybe a thousand years. It was Andy Marston, a nice kid, never in trouble, likeable as all hell, with a big mouth, big teeth, and a big grin. His ears matched the other facial parts. He'd never said "Boo" in town.

Marston applied the same security routine Talmon had used, and then disappeared into the cave.

Four more boys came, and Dobson flashed a mirror and two flashes came back. He waited half an hour and the other stake-out posse members arrived.

Dobson heard their reports, made his report, and then said, "We have to move in fast because there's a backside exit from the cave. I have no idea where it comes out, so we have to get all under control from this end."

It was just after 9 o'clock in the morning when they rushed into the cave, shouting and screaming and scaring the daylights out of the boys milling around in fright and excitement. Dobson had Billy Talmon by the arm, his other hand feeling around his waist for the presence of The Book, which was nowhere in sight.

"Where's The Book?" he demanded.

"It ain't here. I buried it under some rocks. I knew someone was coming." He spoke with clear confidence, past-boy, nearer man than his pals, a deeper tone residing in his voice.

Yet Dobson doubted his words. Thornwell had said The Book was at every meeting; it was what drew the boys, The Book and its immeasurable promise of correction.

Dobson knew he'd have to search the whole cave. Billy Talmon might have had time to chuck it somewhere or might have hidden it when he arrived. The Book had to be here.

"Take them all down to my office," he said as loud as he could.

One of the boys started crying. Talmon stood as tall as the men when he said, "I'm going to show it to the marshal whenever he shows up. We already told him we had something for him."

"How'd you tell him?" Dobson said, still holding him by the arm.

"By telegraph."

"That's okay. We'll check it out," Dobson said, for he had seen the tell-tale flicker cross Billy Talmon's face.

There still was hope, he thought, but we have to find The Book.

"Take them away," he yelled again, "and lock them up."

All the others left the cave, Dobson saying it was up to him to find The Book. If he didn't find it, he'd have to take different measures.

The search was simple. The Book was a cinch to find, on a shelf of rock, but carefully tucked away, in another part of the cave. Dobson, nervous, anxiety almost ready to scream its way free of him, slipped his taught fingers across the leather cover and slowly began to believe he felt some comfort in the touch.

Vaguely, intermittently, he waited for relief to set in.

It came slowly, dragging itself across his chest, the way fire might feed on damp wood.

His name leaped out at him. Then other names, chief citizens of Ross Corners. No women were mentioned, however, and he felt relieved at that revelation.

Two solid hours he spent reading the information, and page by page, after letting the information settle into his mind and then letting it sift away as best he could, fed The Book, by each page

80

he had read, to the fire that Billy Talmon had started for the meeting of The Raggedies.

In the late afternoon, nothing alive in the fire but a few embers, the smell and sight of the burnt leather cover of The Book shifting back and forth in his senses, Sheriff Bill Dobson headed back to Ross Corners in the warmth of the slanting sun. He could not begin to imagine what the rest of the day would bring, but he had a fairly decent idea.

He hoped it was decent.

Coachman's Find

Dutch Plebis yanked back on the reins of the westbound Fremont-Jehrico Stagecoach. "Whoa, horse," he yelled. "Whoa, horse." After a bit of tussling the six-horse team came to a stop almost at the foot of a drop in the road. "D'ju see what I saw, Kirby?"

"I ain't seen nothin' yet, Dutch, what ain't supposed to be where it is. You funnin' me on somethin'?" Kirby, on his first ever stagecoach ride as shotgun, looked all around and saw nothing so different on the road that it would make Dutch Plebis stop the coach.

Plebis stood on top of the coach and took another look. Way out on the grass he saw the woman fall down. "You stay here, Kirby, and keep good rein on 'em. I'll be right back and I ain't about to walk to Fremont. There's a woman out there on the grass. No horse. No cover. No company. I'm goin' out there and get her. Pray she ain't dead. I ain't got time to bury her."

As he climbed down from the rig, aware his passengers had heard him, he said, "You sure that shovel's up there, Kirby?"

"Put it there myself, Dutch." He watched Plebis walk off into the grass.

For the last few feet approaching the woman, Plebis began to say what prayer he knew for the weak and the helpless and the near dead. She looked near dead, pale as linen on the line, dress ripped, the small hands bloody and leaving stains on her dress. The dress had changed to yellow and red, a lot of red.

He touched her throat and found a pulse. "Well, lady, I don't know what got at cha, but I gotta pick you up and tote you back to the wagon. Pardon these old hands intrudin' on you, ma'am, but I gotta hurry at this."

He picked up the unconscious woman and carried her back to the stagecoach, ordered one man topside and put the woman in his place. He turned to one of the two women passengers and said, "Do what you can for her 'til we get to Fremont. She's near dead, I think."

The ride into Fremont was an easy run, without any disturbances bothering Plebis except the condition of the woman … and the cause of it.

He unloaded her at Doc Potter's place next door to the barber shop, telling the doctor just the way he had found her. "She fell down just as I was lookin' at her, Doc. Fell like she had died right in front of me. But I caught her pulse and brung her in instead of buryin' her. I don't even know her name. I'll be back later. I got me a day off comin'."

Plebis returned to the doctor's office a few hours later, his throat wet, the dust gone after a bath in the back of the barbershop. "I feel like a new man, Doc, and I hope the lady does too. How she doin'?"

"Well, Dutch, I'm glad you brought her in when you did. At least we got some more water into her. Near dry as a bone, she was. The ladies on the coach did okay, not giving her too much. I had to hold her back from gulping. Other than that, and getting scared to death by some thugs who jumped her family's wagon, whose situation we don't know yet, she'll be okay. Said she jumped into the bushes 'cause she was on a private matter and heard lots of noise, shouting and stuff, but only one shot. Poor girl doesn't know what happened to her folks."

"Who is she, Doc? You get a name?"

"Yes. She says her name is Millie Ford and she was coming to Fremont and they were going to buy the Drummond place, the Box B spread. Him and a few of his boys and the sheriff are out there now taking a look around. I haven't heard anything yet."

The news, when it did come, was not good for Millie Ford. Her folks and her kid brother dead, one shot and two knifed. Millie Ford was sitting up when Plebis walked in to say hello.

"I'm deep sorry, Ma'am, about your family."

Millie Ford said, "You're the man who found me and brought me in, aren't you? The doctor told me. I guess I'm the saddest girl in the world right now. I don't know what I'm going to do. They say my father's money, what he was going to buy the ranch with, is gone. It was under the wagon, hid away. I had some bad feelings about this right from the beginning. But Ma said it was the best thing Pa could do to get him going again."

She looked around again, and then down at her dress. "Oh, my, what'll I ever do now?" She started crying again.

Plebis put an arm around her and said, "Well, Ma'am, you can stay at my place until you figure out what you're gonna do. Don't let them talk you into working bar at the Black Horse Saloon, and they will try for a new face. Them at the saloon do it every time some lonesome gal comes through here. Most of them stay right where they put them. You don't want any of that, Ma'am."

"The doctor told me you thought I was dead."

83

"I sure did, Ma'am. You collapsed out there like you was shot. We'd hadda bury you. Couldn't leave you out there. No Ma'am. Not out there, even if I was late gettin' in by a whole lot."

Plebis, with some advice from Doc Potter about caring for Millie Ford, took her to his small cabin at the edge of town, where the road comes in from Jehrico and elsewhere down the line. It was very modest, a man's place from the first look, but Millie Ford said, "I will do what I can while I'm here, Dutch. I can cook and sew and tend garden. I can ride a horse and shoot a gun and throw a rope. I've done it since I was a kid. My father was waiting for my brother to grow up and do it for him, but he had to teach me in the meantime."

Plebis said, "That sure pleases an old bachelor, Ma'am. You got the run of the place. I'll make sure I don't get in your way, but I ain't here much. I'll sleep in the shack out back."

"No way," Millie said. "I'm not a blushing girl, Dutch. You make your bed and I'll make mine. I'm not kicking you out of your house. But there's one thing I wish you'd do for me. Go out there and look around the place where my folks were killed and robbed. I think you have some good sense about you. See what you can find. I am very suspicious about the whole thing."

"I'll do that, Millie. Tell me where the money was hid. I'll start from there."

Plebis went to see the sheriff. "You find anythin' out there, Sheriff?"

"Not a thing, Dutch. Me and Drummond's boy went clean all over everything, and saw nothing that we could latch onto, about who might have done it. We got the folks buried without the girl seeing them. The shot one, the father, was quick and clean, thank goodness, but the mother and the boy were knifed awful bad. I'm glad she never saw them."

"Well, I'm goin' out there to take a look. Girl asked me to."

"Good hunting, Dutch, but not much left. The wagon's pretty old and broken up. Might just rot out there if someone takes the wheels off'n it."

Plebis found Kirby in the Black Horse Saloon and said, "Let's take a ride, Kirby. We got some checkin' to do for Millie."

"Sure, Dutch. She doin' okay?"

"For now, yes."

At the site they found that scavengers had taken much of the Ford's property. Even the canvas was taken off the wagon,

84

one wheel was gone and an old stump was holding the wagon level.

Kirby said, "They don't waste much time, do they, Dutch?"

"They don't got much to start with and I figure they don't have much more now, those scavengers, like the buzzards they are. The ones who took the money, they got somethin' now, that's who. Let's look around."

From Millie's description, Plebis looked under the wagon. He called to Kirby, "Take a look at this, Kirby."

He pointed to the underside of the wagon. "Millie said her father hid the money on top of one of these boards and banged it back in place. One of these six boards. What do you see?"

"Well," Kirby said, "I see only one board broke where it was pulled down. It's like the third one from the front."

"The only one?" Plebis said.

"Yuh, the only one."

"What's that tell you, Kirby?"

"Tells me plain out they wasn't goin' to waste any time on them other boards."

"Meanin'?"

"Meanin' they knew where the money was even before they got here."

"Who knew they were comin'?" Plebis had lowered his eyes and was looking right into Kirby's eyes.

"Far as I know, just Drummond and his folk, less'n he told some others. I never heard anything'"

"Let's go sit with the sheriff and think this out for keeps," Plebis said, climbing back into his saddle, looking once more at the scene, certainly glad that Millie Ford did not have a chance to see any of it, the shock of robbery and shooting and noise making her wander, get lost, get found.

Plebis was going to tell the sheriff everything he'd come across, including his suspicions, but changed his mind at the last minute. "Tell me what you folks did out there at the site of the killin', Sheriff."

"We looked over things pretty close."

"Look under the wagon?" Plebis said.

"Not me. Drummond looked it over and said he saw nothing out of the ordinary under there. You see anything that bothered you, Dutch?"

Plebis told him the conversation he and Kirby had, every detail of it.

"Makes Drummond look pretty bad, but we have to have more than that. He could have been plain lazy under the wagon, or did not see what difference a broken board would make. "I'd be kind of dumb about it myself."

Plebis thought a while and said, "Let me take a poke at this, Sheriff. I got this information to you, but I'd like to do some more. That girl Millie is plain busted up about it. She don't say much, but she wears it all over herself. She's a fine girl and I'd do everythin' I can for her, includin' at the saloon on Saturday night when Drummond comes into town."

"You got it, Dutch, so ride with it. Don't seem like enough to do anything with it, but it's worth a try."

Saturday evening, dusk settled in, his chores around the house done, Plebis rounded the corner and heard, then saw, the commotion in front of the saloon.

Kirby was sitting on his butt in the dusty road, and a bunch of Drummond's cow hands on the saloon walk in laughing at him.

"You keep shootin' off your mouth, buster, and you'll get more than this. Don't try to rope us in on some damned killin'." He raised his hands and ushered the gang back into the saloon. Plebis knew him as Mike Jordan, Drummond's foreman.

Plebis was disturbed two ways. "What happened, Kirby? You shoot your mouth off about what we found? Did you? Answer me."

"Honest, Dutch, I just told the Drummond foreman they missed what we found at the site of the killin's."

"D'ju tell 'em what it was?"

"Course not. I wouldn't do that, Dutch. Drummond don't need no break from me."

"Let's go back in and see what's cookin' with 'em. Drummond there yet?" Plebis looked along the hitch rail at the row of horses tied off as if he was looking for Drummond's mount.

"Not yet, Dutch, but some of his boys said he's comin'. Always comes on Saturday night like he runs the show for the evenin'."

Jordan, Drummond's top hand, looked up from his place at the bar and said, "Hey, Dutchie boy, I see you found your shotgun on his butt out front, deserved it, comin' in here and tellin' us we was part of them murders. We'll throw him out again if he says anymore."

86

Plebis faced right up to him. "What do you do if the sheriff comes in here and locks up your boss, and maybe some of you, for killin' them folks? How's that sit with you, Mike?

"You want to get thrown out, too, Dutchie? I can arrange that easy." Jordan moved menacingly away from the bar, giving himself room for an expected confrontation with Plebis.

The stage driver had another set to his mind. "Hey, there, Mike. I guess you'll do it your way. That's if you want to be part of the gang that goes to the penitentiary and sits there until the sun don't shine no more? You really willin' to do that? Stick up for someone who knifed a woman and a kid of 12? A decent woman and her 12 year-older? That goes for your whole crowd. Take a good last look at some of them if that's the way you want it."

He pointed around the room, "Them's a lot of Box-B boys and if they want what's comin' with murderin' a woman and her kid, let 'em tell you they're stayin' in place with you. Put your chops onto that, Mike."

Jordan shrank a little from that threatening picture as he perceived a decided change in some of the Box-B cow hands. The change was instantly obvious, the popular thrust of camaraderie and one-for-all and all-for-one mode of operation suddenly rent by division, by indecision. He spun on his heels and said, "What're you goin' to do? You got proof of all this?"

Plebis was quick with him, seeing the changes coming on the whole crew. "You willin' to find out the truth?"

Jordan's face said he was thinking over all the implications and all the possibilities. "I ain't gonna hide anythin' from the law. Do what you gotta do." The threat of a penitentiary stay had set solidly on his face.

The mood in the Black Horse Saloon had made a wide swing from the Drummond influence. Plebis saw it immediately, knowing what influence Drummond had put upon the town from the beginning. He could see it in the room; the banker, in a far corner with a couple of cronies, was a Drummond pal, and the owner of the general store had Drummond as his best customer. Even the bartender was an old Drummond cow hand who couldn't hack the drive anymore and was put behind the bar at Drummond's request.

He knew he'd have a tough sell once things got going, but he found hard pictures in his mind of a horrible crime. Then he saw an image of Millie Ford, out on the grass, looking as if she was dead, the blood spread on her dress.

It steeled him with resolve.

As Drummond walked into the saloon an hour later, the place went silent. A shade under six feet, he cast a healthy shadow, with wide shoulders, hefty biceps in a loose gray shirt, and a vigilance caught up in his eyes. He looked around the saloon and saw his whole crew. His smile initially said a secure sense was working in him.

Plebis was reading signs.

"Hey, Mike," Drummond said to his foreman, "you ready for a good night on the town? Tell the boys to belly-up 'cause I'm buying all of them some drinks." He threw some greenbacks down on the counter. The bartender scooped up the bills, put them in the cash draw, and poured a healthy first round for the boys of the Box-B. A few of them drank their beer quickly, as if a second round would follow in a hurry.

Plebis saw a few of them quite hesitant at drinking, looking at their glasses, possibly measuring connections, penalties, guilt of some sort.

But when Drummond put his arm across the shoulders of Jordan, he felt the signs of indifference, and then stiffened himself as he saw Dutch Plebis approaching him. Drummond's face reflected his sudden awareness of things being out of kilter.

Plebis was direct in his speech. "Drummond, I heard you and your boys here were part of the gang that checked out the Ford killin' site, where the father was shot and the mother and a 12-year old son were knifed like a wild and ornery butcher went to work on them."

Drummond, drawing in Plebis's statement as relief from the sudden apprehension received from Jordan, stepped in gladly. "Well, Dutch, we did what we could. Helped out the sheriff as much as possible. Not much to be seen though. I suspect some madman had been there and done all that. It was a mess, I agree." He drank off his beer in one gulp.

Plebis saw his hand shake a little as he put the glass on the bar.

Drummond said, "I heard you were on the site a couple of times. Didn't find much, did you? We didn't find a thing other than a plain horror." A bit of ease had settled into his voice. Plebis caught that too.

Plebis said, "I hope you folks that went out there with the sheriff checked everything out."

"We did."

"I hope someone checked under the wagon, and the front seat of the wagon." Plebis felt like he was loading a rifle at the shooting range.

Drummond said, "We saw nothing on the seat of the wagon. Couple of my boys did that. I saw them. And I looked under the wagon myself. Nothing there. Nothing at all."

The single pearl of sweat rolled on Drummond's forehead, directly under the brim of his hat, and dripped down one cheek. With the back of his hand, he brushed it off quickly.

"D'ju see a broken board down under there?" Plebis put a dumbfounded look on his face.

"Oh, yeh, but it must have been broken before or during the fight."

Plebis put another round in the imaginary chamber. "Six cross boards down there and only one broken? That didn't hit you kinda funny?"

"What's a single board say about anything? Could have happened a hundred ways."

"I'll tell you one way," Plebis said. "It was the only one broken by the killer 'cause he knowed there was money hidden there. The money Ford was goin' to buy your ranch with."

"How'd anybody know that?" Drummond said, as the second pearl in the guilty chain started to fall in place on his forehead.

"The Ford daughter told me. I found her out there. She's a witness to everythin' that happened. And she saw her father hide that money up on top of that board and only the family and a helper knew. That helper told someone who turned out to be a killer and a thief and a dirty rat as bad as one can get in this rotten life."

"Not much I can do about that. We looked over the scene for any signs and we didn't find any. Can't blame us for missing something. We did our best."

The "We" approach of Drummond had made a move on his crew. Plebis, still good at reading signs, saw Jordan shrink visibly each time Drummond said "we."

"Maybe you don't know that the daughter had a list of the green backs her father hid, a whole list that the banker gave them

89

when Ford cleaned out his savings from the bank, every last dollar."

Plebis saw two things at the same time. He saw Drummond's hand make a slight move toward his pocket, and then it stopped, and another pearl, then another, made their way in the chain of beads coming off his forehead.

And behind the bar, he saw the bartender slip his hand into the cash box and take out the last greenbacks put there, those from Drummond spent when he bought the rounds for his crew. The bartender put the bills in his pocket.

At that point, the sheriff walked in and stood in the middle of the saloon, his hand on his pistol. He said, "What's going on here, boys? We got some kind of stand-off? Fella came out and told me I ought to be in here."

"It's like this, Sheriff," Plebis said, "We know the numbers on the greenbacks that was stolen from Millie's parents. And someone's got that money. And Drummond here just bought a round for his crew and paid in greenbacks and that money was put in the cash box. When I told folks here about it, Shortlick there, the bartender who used to work for Drummond, took it out of the cash box and stuck it in his own pocket. You go take a look in his pocket, Sheriff and see if I ain't tellin' the truth."

A number of men made moves in the next second: Shortlick went to get rid of the money; Drummond went for his gun; Mike Jordan, long-time foreman of the Box-B, almost taken in by a crude, maniacal boss and killer, jumped his boss from behind and wrapped his arms around him."

There was, of course, no known bill numbers, all a ruse put on by Plebis. Someone, he knew, knew the location of the money. Someone who saw the broken board must have broken it to take the money. Drummond had ignored the broken board and had admittedly seen it. All of it pointed back at the owner of the Box-B Ranch who knew how much Ford was going to pay for the ranch. Plebis had played it his own way.

The judge, when Drummond was convicted and hanged for the murders and the robbery, awarded the Box-B Ranch to Millie Ford, with not a single dissent from anybody in the town of Fremont.

Dutch Plebis became her foreman and Kirby was his top hand, after a while.

Mike Jordan and some of the crew left and were never heard from again. A few stayed at the ranch with the new boss, trying to make amends for their ineptness but not their guilt.

Not too much time passed before Dutch Plebis, stagecoach driver, one-time detective and mystery solver, picked up in his arms and carried Millie Ford for the second time, this time over the threshold of the door to their home.

Secret of the Cave

Mountain Jackson, no other name known by the few men he met in the mountains or saw at re-supply time or pelt trading, was bigger than his mule, a stubborn but hard-worker, the only kind of an animal that Jackson would lavish any affection on. "You smell that sweet water, Hildy? Smell it like I do? Up here's someplace hidin' on us. You be still here and I'll have a look around. 'Bout time we had a treat."

With his great fur coat doffed and sitting across Hildy's back for an airing, and his rifle in one hand, the big man stared at the walls of the escarpment sweeping in a half circle, and the mass of rocks piled at the base like Mother Nature had set out to cover her tracks at some kind of mischief. At 4000 feet, the land had changed, and underground water he hoped followed a flow hidden from the eyes of any man for over a thousand years.

Jackson and his mule had run out of water the day before and the pinch had slipped in on them as they climbed into this high canyon. He tied Hildy to a rock big enough to hold her. "You be still, girl. Don't go nosin' around. I don't know what I'd do without you. Your feet are so sure, girl, you could dance at a barn dance and I'd be your partner. I'll damned well find some water for us'n's."

With a pat at Hildy's backside, Jackson headed for the base of a major rock fall, at the foot of a steep wall, looking as if it had not moved in a thousand years. In a dark recess pinned against the wall he saw an opening that promised further excitement. He urged his big frame toward that next spot, even as he felt the shift in air, the sense of freshness in the current, and knowing he'd have to light a torch before long. The new air carried both the essence of water in it and the aspect of morning when you know it's going to be a good day.

It was near high noon, he realized, when two things happened; in the heart of the cave he heard water dripping steadily, and in a sudden shaft of light from directly overhead saw a man-made object, its square shape distinctive as it could be, sitting on a shelf of rock where the shaft of light, overhead sunshine, fell on it for a few seconds and then departed. It was as if the light was withdrawn up a long shaft right through the heart of the mountain.

Jackson saw the spot at once as marked by some man before him who had also experienced the shaft of light and where it hit at high noon. "Got to be checkin' that out, old boy," he said aloud, his voice sounding again from deeper in the cave.

But the surprise finding was second thought with him as he thought about Hildy being as thirsty as he was. With a bit of agility about him, he followed the sound of dripping water, to where it came out of a crevice above his head and fell directly below into a small crater, which in turn flowed over its far side and dropped again to a lower level, that level out of sight.

He collected two full canteens, enjoyed some himself, and proceeded to tend to Hildy's thirst. Over a fire against one wall he made coffee and heated a piece of meat for himself and gave some oats to his mule. Under a ledge he set up his bed for the coming night and brought Hildy as close as he could. When the stars popped up over the peaks about him, climbing as if they were on a steep incline, toting all the majesty with them that he ever craved, he crawled toward sleep. There were times he had lost his breath at such views that had broadened overhead, the wonder of that awful power pulling on him from limitless space, the wonder of their constant and permanent travels as if in the very beginning they had been commissioned for such tasks, all born and bred for such beauty. His choice of a mountain life when he was but a boy of 16 was absolute, caught up as he was in the heavenly powers come evident to him. The skies, he avowed, especially the night skies, are better observed the closer you are to them.

After such appreciations he began thinking at length what might be in the container on the shelf in the cave that only high noon could find for the eyes of a man.

"It t'weren't born there, Hildy," he said, as much to comfort his mule as to entertain himself a bit. The mule answered with a soft bray, in accord with the tone of Jackson's voice. "Might be some weapons and some ammo, old girl, or a clutch of gold, or a gone family's lifetimes all gathered up in one nutshell. If I was a bettin' man, I'd bet on the last particular, girl."

He felt sleep touching him. "It has to be valuable, some ways," he said aloud, letting his words drift off on the night air. Sleep came deeper upon him as he thought about all the possibilities, of what was in the container and how it had been placed there. The visions and images rolled through him and brought him to his sleep. The mountain music began even as he dozed off, the music of his life, bird cries, owl hoots, domain seekers or markers like wolves and coyotes and the innocuous yap

93

of a mother fox calling her young back to her side. It was music for a loner. An owl was plaintive, a coyote more so, notes of the grand music.

It was only a lone bird somewhere and Hildy's morning music that wakened him in the pre-dawn mix of grays so different that he could tell time by them. "An hour's sun-up, Hildy, and we get to eatin' and explorin' a bit more. I got no hurry in me, girl, less'n I lose some of this magic the good Lord's waving' at me like he allus does." Looking again at the early sky, still some stars available for wonder, he nodded slowly and patted his mule.

Repeating the almost the same meal from the night before, he added a dry onion into the skittle and near burnt it through. Coffee aroma and onion gone black surged freely into the canyon, enough, he thought, to wake any unknown visitors in the area. He kept his ears alert for any new sound.

Early morning passed through his survival ritual of caring for what took care of him, his animal, his gear, his supplies, lastly his self. With the area cleaned up after breakfast, he lit a torch from the fire and hastened into the cave. Rolling three rocks together, one on top of two, he managed to get one hand into the box after he pried the cover off with little difficulty. He did not want to move the box from its secret place. Papers came into hand, a small soft bag he hoped was gold dust, a few loose coins, and more papers. In one corner he felt a pistol grip, then the trigger mechanism, and the long barrel. By touch he knew what it was, a Colt .45 single action Buntline revolver with a barrel about a foot long. He had seen and handled one with deep curiosity in the village below the Snake River the year before, in the holster of a posse leader.

In the soft bag was enough gold dust to take care of Mountain Jackson for a few years if he lived in a village or settlement down below; much longer if he stayed in the mountains with few visits to civilization. The coins, in gold, amounted to more than $300. One of the papers was a letter, one was a final will and testament of a man named Jacob Grimes, and one was an ink sketch of a little girl, pretty as her picture, dimpled, curly hair, eyes like stars and a smile to match. And Jackson was absolutely correct about the Buntline Special, the barrel almost like a rifle barrel, near long as his forearm.

On a rock he sat, Hildy not far away, the silence now and then like a musical accompaniment. It was a perfect place to read the letter:

Whoever finds my last leavings, by the grace of God they be found. I am Jacob Grimes, once of Butler, Pennsylvania, once bound for Montana but got nowhere near, according to my estimate. I was attacked and pursued into these mountains by brigands on foot. They fired upon me several times, killed one of my mules, near got me a few times. I found this cave and placed all my possessions in this box that I found under a ledge down below and could not leave it behind me, and leave my last will and testament within the box. Who finds me will find water here also, which is the only way I was able to outlast my pursuers, who most likely ran out of water and withdrew their attack. I will try to get out of here in the darkness, hoping they have really gone, and get to a town of any size.

I left my wife and little girl in Butler to seek a place in Montana my brother owned, but he never advised me if it was suitable for me and my family. I believe he has died and left it to me. I came alone rather than drag my darlings with me on what may be a fruitless journey, but one I had to take.

Then Jackson read the will of Jacob Grimes:

To the person who finds the accompanying note and this will and all my personal leavings, I, Jacob Grimes, leave one half of these possessions if and when he delivers the other half to my wife and child, MaryLouise Grimes, my wife of 7 years, and my daughter Rosemary, 5 years of age, in Butler, Pennsylvania. Signed this unknown day in summer of 1879, by Jacob Grimes, sound and hale for the moment.

Jackson, staring at the little girl's pretty face in the ink sketch, knowing she would grow to be a beautiful woman, mother and daughter full of good memories of a good time, felt a surge pound through his huge frame. There was something besides the mountains, the night sky and awesome stars, the moon like a good witch on a good night. There was promise. A deed to be done. A promise to be made. A quest to be undertaken.

It boiled over in him.

He patted Hildy on the rump and said, "Girl, we are goin' on a long, long walk."

Jackson packed in his saddle bags what he thought was of value in the box, including the will, the last note, the coins and

95

the bag of gold dust, the sketch of Rosemary, and a map of an unknown location. The map contained very little text and showed a mountain range, two rivers meeting, and a few sketched figures completely foreign to Jackson. He assumed Grimes was a decent sketch artist. The Buntline Special was tucked in his waistband, fitting there as if it was made for him.

He made a thorough search of the area for Grimes, or his body, and found nothing. He searched for two solid days, thinking about Grimes' wife and little girl back in Pennsylvania.

Mountain Jackson, finally setting out on the mission with his mule, had never felt as confident as the day broke, the stars leaped away from his grasp, and the route he took lead downhill, out of the mountain chain.

Four months later, September's sun still about, leaves at least a week or two before the colors began their appearance, he was near Butler, Pennsylvania. Hildy was worn out, he was tired, and he pitched his place beside a small stream. In the morning, after a sleep only reached after the stars touched him again, he bathed in the stream, cleaned up his general looks, washed meager clothes in the stream and strung them on warm rocks under the rays of the sun. Two passersby laughed at him, and at Hildy standing on the banking looking nothing but lazy.

An hour or so later a sheriff came by and asked him where he was going and gave Jackson directions to the Grimes home, "It's a bare cabin set back off this stream on the far side of town, which will come at you up that road over there." He pointed to the north and added, "She's a nice lady whose husband went west for fortune but she hasn't heard from him at all since he left. Only reason I came by is a few folks saw you sleeping here and said you looked strange, but I guess you been out there, ain't you?" He pointed west this time, the hungry look of a man too nestled in one place running across his face.

"I been there a time, Sheriff, working in the mountains, free with the birds and critters spawned there 'fore I got there. I got news for the lady. Been a hunk of year getting' this far with it."

"Ain't bad, is it?" the sheriff said, "'cause she is a good sort, as I meant."

"What I got for her in news ain't bad, Sheriff, but what I don't know might be."

"You didn't see her husband out there?"

"No, but I got word for her that I'll deliver personal, if you don't mind me sayin' so."

"Not a bit, mister. I was just checking, way some folks are hereabouts. You have a good day."

He rode off on his black horse with a trot Jackson figured would have made his journey in half the time it took, Hildy being what she was.

It was the little girl who advised him he was at the end of his journey, as she stood in front of the little cabin, which was as plain as a spoke on a wheel. The sketch could have been alive in his hand, he thought, but instead was alive right in front of him; pretty as her picture he had looked at again this morning, dimpled, curly hair, eyes like stars and a smile to match. The smile stretched wider as he smiled back, his own eyes bright as stars, his beard like solid black clouds.

Jackson, alighting from Hildy, said, "I bet your name is Rosemary and my girl here, my mule, her name is Hildy. Is your mother about?"

"Hi Hildy," the little girl said, "My name is Rosemary. My mom's name is MaryLouise. What's your name, mister?"

"Real friends, what there are, call me Homer, but I ain't been called that in 25 years. Please ask your mother to come out and see me."

"She's sewing things now. She doesn't like to be away from it. Gets mad at me sometimes." The smile was still working for her, but she ran, calling out for her mother. "A big man is here to see you and he's with his girl, Hildy."

A tall, thin, obviously overworked woman came out the door of the cabin. She was pleasant looking, had some of Rosemary in her face, and carried a piece of cloth she was working on. Her dress was simple and buttoned to the neck, and was made of strange material. Her eyes were blue-green, her nose was shapely as were her lips, and there was a particular grace in her slightest movements. She made Jackson think of what Grimes must have been like to corral such a woman. He said "lucky" under his breath and then immediately changed his mind, saying "knowing," not knowing what he meant but having an idea of keenness.

"May I help you, sir?" she said, her voice light, belying the tired look about her person. "I have some food I can spare, but not much. We live thinly here, Rosemary and I, until my husband gets back." She didn't say where he was, where he went, or what time he would be back.

"Ma'am, Mrs. Grimes, my name is Homer Jackson and I have been four months on the road coming here from out there." He looked over his shoulder and nodded west, "Out there in the mountains."

"Did you see my husband out there?" The light was in her eyes, and the hope.

"No, Ma'am. But I come acrost what he left behind in a safe place, safe until I come acrost it in a strange fashion. But I think he was in trouble from some men and he put his valuables aside, hid them well, hopin' somebody like me would find 'em and get them here to you. I have a note from him, his last will and testament, some coin and gold, and a sketch of your daughter that must have been his best property of all. I found them in a cave in the high mountains. I went lookin' for him, spent a few days at it, but never come across a sign of him at all. I have no idea what happened to him. But I brought all this stuff back, as he wanted."

"Oh," she said, "please do come in and talk with us. Bring what you brought to us. We will have supper together. You are most welcome, Mr. Jackson."

After tending Hildy, my mule, I'll be right along, Ma'am. She got me this far and deserves the best I can swarm up for her."

"We have a few apples we can spare. You are welcome to them."

They sat and even before they had looked at the things Jackson had brought from her husband, she fed him.

After the meal they sat across the kitchen and he showed them all he had.

He showed her the note first, then the will and the sketch. Her eyes filled with tears as she read the note and the will and looked at the sketch.

"Oh," she said, "I never saw this sketch. He did have a fine hand. This is beautiful. He caught her full spirit."

She did not know what to make of the map, and shrugged her shoulders. "I do not understand any of it."

He put the gold dust in her hands and the coins, all there but a few he had spent on the way. "I can account on all that's missing, Ma'am. Every penny. Least I could do."

"Oh, Rosemary, what joy. We do not have to work for all the neighbors like we have. Now we can breathe. Now we can eat proper. Now we can think about heading west to find your father."

To Jackson she said, "Half of all is yours, Mister Jackson, and if you are willing, and I know you are that brand of man, I'll pay wages if you can get us to that place in Montana that my husband mentioned."

"I'll do that, Ma'am, with you knowin' we might not ever find him. He was in some serious trouble to go to all the trouble he did about this here gear." He spread his hand over the top of the table.

Rosemary was looking at the map, staring at it before her whole face bloomed with intelligence.

"I know these. I saw them in daddy's book." She was pointing to the strange symbols on the map, the ones that Jackson could not understand.

She retrieved the book from a 3-book shelf in a corner of the kitchen, and showed them to Jackson.

Jackson in turn lit up as he said, "They tell me he found gold, Ma'am, found gold out there in the mountains and these symbols on the map tell me where. These are his clues. I know what he means. Before we get to Montana, Ma'am, we'll do a little minin' on our own."

MaryLouise Grimes hugged Homer Jackson, the kind of hug he had not known since he was a child. It went right through him the way the nightly stars did.

Outside an owl hooted from some high place, a dog barked in the distance not quite the sound of a coyote or wolf, and Hildy brayed awareness of a farther reach working on her as well.

Jackson knew it all.

Doc Hannah Goes to Town

The small sign, hardly visible from the road, said, "Wm. Hannah, MD." It was hand-painted, almost saying so by the quality of the script, loose, off-hand, all things tolerable. And Doc didn't wear a tie, never wore a suit, wanted nothing ornate in a life that touched life and death, sometimes in turn. The only doctor "near to town" was thirty-five on his next birthday, unmarried, "as good looking as a man can get," one woman had said in Caliper, Texas, a mile or so down the road. He was a born Texan, sent east by his parents to discover new things on the horizon, found doctoring, came back to settle about 100 miles from home.

"How come you haven't moved into town yet, Doc?" Greg Thormond the banker, who often had to size up people in a hurry, sat his horse at Doc Hannah's front door.

Thormond knew the answer before it came from Hannah, sitting on the porch waving a cup of coffee in his hand as if it was saying something to the point in question. Aromas, settling about the banker, were almost visible. He'd had been looking at the spread of Doc's garden alongside the house, flowering the rail fence all the way in from the road to Doc's private paradise, noting the clean corners of the small barn beyond a vegetable plot green and lush. There was no clutter about, no debris waiting on energy, no space wasted. Wind rustled in the trees. An early summer smell of honeysuckle blessed the air. He wondered if he could enjoy the place without the constant demands and pains of the bank. He decided he could, though he knew Doc Hannah had perils of his own; strange wounds on patients, late night callers, the mystery of doctor and patient knowledge, potential threats of any order.

"No dance hall out here, Greg. No saloon. No shooting on Saturday nights without fail, though I've heard a few shots from a distance now and then. Rifle fire. Maybe hunters after peccary in the gorge." The coffee cup pointed out to the north.

Thormond had heard it all before. And now he thought the doctor looked ten years younger than he was. Maybe more. "He's found some secret out here, grass all around, a clump of trees, a spread of prairie flowers," came to him as an unsought statement.

"I'll see you tonight, Doc. Game starts at 7 o'clock; soon as Clara clears the table. It's her favorite night, too. Tells me all the time she's glad the doctor comes to play cards with the others."

"Yeh," said Hannah, "like they'll be gunshots from cheaters."

"Hell, Doc, there's not a good shot in the crowd. None of us could hit a mule if he was sitting on the gun sight."

"You didn't say anything about cheaters."

"Hell, we know Harry'd cheat in a minute if he thought he could get away with it."

"The mark of a frugal freight owner, wouldn't you say?"

"No indecision with you, Doc, is there?" He'd never heard Doc Hannah say, "I don't know or I don't know about that." About anything that came up in conversation.

"Not in this game," Hannah said, pointing at the sign that was a standard as well as a statement all on its own.

At five minutes past 7 o'clock the six long-time poker players sat down at the banker's dining table. He had wanted to get a real poker table but his wife wouldn't budge on the issue. "This is not a casino Greg, no matter how many games you play here. But I am glad you can get the doctor here. The man is good company; doesn't get locked up in the town's messes or rumors. Strictly on an even keel. Out in the kitchen I can hear him carry on about things. Did you ask him again about moving into town?"

"Had the same answer, Clara. Same as before. There doesn't seem to be a thing that will budge him."

"Doesn't he ever speak about women? Mention any of them? There are half a dozen sweet eligibles that would jump at the chance of spending time with him."

"Doc doesn't talk about patients, women, youngsters, old folks, and tradesmen that deal with him. That includes the livery, the undertaker, the carriage maker, the hotel owner, the saloon boss. I guess that takes care of everybody. None of them, not on a bet."

She put her hands on her hips. "I know that from the kitchen on game night, Greg, but what about elsewhere? What does he talk about out there, out on the prairie riding that horse of his, having a drink with a friend like Bill Grissom at the store, or Harvey at the forge making those little tools he likes, those special pincers and knives? Nothing come out of that? Is he all mystery?"

"When it's all said and done, Clara, he's the best doc we could ever have. Bill Smithers would have lost a leg if it wasn't for Doc, and Mabel Sanders got that little baby girl of hers because Doc stayed with her for three days."

"That was his longest stay in town, ever," she replied, a smile crossing her face.

The game that evening was in its late stages, Thormond slightly ahead in winnings, Doc Hannah nodding at each loss, the other players were neutral and level.

A crashing sound came from the front porch. The door burst open and a young man yelled, "Hurry, Doc, Bert Harbors' boy Teddy's been mangled by a runaway. He's real hurtin'."

Doc Hannah, grabbing his bag by the door, was running down Caliper's main street, following the young man calling him on. "Down here, Doc, down by the livery." The doctor, bag and all, kept pace with him.

A good-sized crowd had gathered. One woman was leaning over the ten-year old boy when Hannah knelt beside her. "He's in bad shape, Doc. Said everything hurt before he passed out again. Blood everywhere, you'll see."

Hannah, noting things, checked the boy for vital signs. He stood up and pointed to two men in front of the crowd, "Get some boards for a litter. Hurry. Try the livery, out back. Strip them down if you have to." He pointed at another man and said, "They might need some tools. Get a hammer and a pry bar for them. In the livery. On the big shelf."

Then, his voice changing again, he addressed the crowd. "Who's got the nearest bed, with a water pump nearby, room for me to work?" He was not being solicitous.

"My place, Doc," the freighter's wife said. She pointed across the road. "I'll go on ahead. You got Harry's and my bed. We'll sleep in Beth's room. She'll go to Amie's house." She ran ahead as two men came from behind the livery with two wide boards. In minutes they had Teddy Harbors in the freighter's bed. "I'll make a pot of coffee," the freighter's wife said. Her name was Nellie. She put a pot of coffee on the outside stove and lit the fire.

Teddy Harbors, for 19 days, lived at the hands of Doc Hannah, in the bed of Nellie and Harry Neville. He had two broken legs, busted ribs, a broken collarbone, one wrist mangled as bad as Doc Hannah had ever seen. He'd been unconscious for the first two days as the doctor worked on him. Hannah admired the young boy without reservation.

"You're tough, Teddy. You haven't cried in three days," he said at one point. "I know you're hurting, your folks too, but we got a leg up on the whole thing." He managed a laugh and the boy, looking at one leg in a splint, laughed with him. Hannah could have hugged the boy, who grimaced again, as he had many times.

Ever observant Greg Thormond, scene watcher, measurer of people and their actions and reactions, saw the romance begin, a small sputter, a match flicker in the far night, a breath of air. Beth Neville, daily watching Hannah minister to Teddy Harbors, marveled at his efficiency, at his attention to details, at his adaptability when he ordered or designed or had made by the blacksmith or the undertaker's assistant a set of tools special for his current patient. He never left the boy's side. The wings of his being beat about Beth every one of those days, and even into her lonely nights at her friend's house down the road. Before long she was there to make breakfast for Doc Hannah, and they would sit on the small porch and share the morning between his visits inside to minister to his patient.

Across the street, in his office, Greg Thormond saw all and smiled. He could feel the small excitement within himself as he remembered his courting days, how they had started even before he knew they were well under way.

"What are you watching, boss?" his teller said one morning.

"Oh, a bit of love in the air, that's all."

"You're right about that, boss. Doc Hannah plain don't leave that boy for a minute. He's a special man."

"He sure is," Thormond replied, "and getting specialer all the time." His smile went right on past the teller, still nodding his head in admiration.

Hannah never knew that every day he was tending Teddy Harbors, town folk were tending his gardens, watering, weeding as needed, keeping the whole place neat the way the doc did. He had no idea having other things on his mind … the care and improvement in his patient for starters, and waiting, eventually, for each morning as Beth Neville would dance around the corner and come into his view.

Greg Thormond and his wife Clara, whom he had alerted to the romance, shared it all from a distance, happy for the pair.

"She's so young," Clara said one morning.

"So were you," Thormond replied.

"Uh huh," she said, hugging his arm. "Young all the way." They laughed in a happy unison.

Came the morning, with reports Teddy had gotten out of bed a few times for exercises, when Thormond saw Beth place her hand on top of Doc Hannah's hand on the small table on the porch. Neither had touched their coffee for half an hour or so. The doc didn't move his hand for a long time. Two days later, it was the doc's hand that did the touching. Thormond knew Doc Hannah had been bitten deep. He could practically hear the announcement.

That afternoon, passersby saw Teddy Neville sitting on the porch, the sun angling down on top of him as if he was being inspected. Some of those passing immediately thought about Doc Hannah's being in town for almost a month; some of them had worked on his property, which gave them a good feeling.

In the early evening, as the sun danced redness on the far mountain tops, Doc Hannah and Beth Neville mounted their horses and rode out of town, headed for his place.

He said, "I don't know what it's going to look like, Beth. It seems like it's been forever since I pulled a weed, brought water for the plants, did anything useful."

"Oh, I won't mind whatever shape it's in," Beth said, not saying a word about the maintenance done in the past month, knowing the complete story, right down to the names of those who had participated.

When they came up the lane, off the main road, Doc Hannah immediately knew what had taken place. "Somebody besides us has taken interest in the old place, Beth. It looks spotless, and hale," he added, looking at his flowers and vegetable garden. "It also says we'll spend our lives here. We sure won't have to move into town after all this."

"Won't bother me a bit," she said, hugging him as the smell of flowers came from all edges of the place, "and you can still go play poker whenever you want."

Shooter in Buckskin

Stories are still told in the mountains of Utah, Wyoming and Colorado and in many ranges that connect with high outposts, how the shooter in buckskin always came out ahead in shooting matches. He'd show up on the day of a shoot, nobody knowing how he found out, and drop his gear at the shooting site and wait for things to get going.

The man, dressed head to toe in buckskin, answered to any and all names, as if saying he was all of them, at least to those speaking to him. Most people, wanting for his real name, just called him Buckskin.

"He's Jim Bridger kin," one speaker said in Churchfree Village, "has to be." The village was halfway up one rugged chain of hills where pelts of many animals made the trading block. It was 1876 and legendary Jim Bridger, great mountain man, had come through the area more than 30 years earlier, picking his way from hide to pelt, getting goods and ammo in return, and a good jug of whiskey. The mountains, every nook and cranny of them, belonged to Jim Bridger. Even had a place named after him, Fort Bridger. Now the mountains seemed to belong to this new phenomenon of the high grounds. Not one person ever said they had an idea of where he had come from.

"Bridger rolled around up here for 10 or 20 years, the way I heard. Must have some leavings hereabouts." The nod of his head was supposed to be enlightening, but didn't come off that way.

The speaker was looking down the narrow road through the village as the buckskin-clad shooter had appeared from a rugged twist in the road, pelts piled on his mule in tow. "He's as good a hunter as he is a shooter," the speaker said. "Must have a hundred traps out there, he catches so much." The pelts, piled high, were from different animals, and looked like a hunchback sitting a tall saddle.

Almost in the middle of those words, a rider came galloping into town, yelling for the sheriff, "Sheriff! Sheriff! Joe Collier's dead out on the trail. Shot in the back. Bushwhacked. Deadshot Joe Collier. He must have been coming in for the shoot." He leaped off his horse, still yelling about his discovery and a small crowd began to gather.

"Poor Joe," Sheriff Phil Wallace said to the rider. "He was a pretty good guy, for a lonely old cuss, and stood as good a

105

chance as anybody in the shoot. Him and Buckskin and that other big fellow from Hell's Bed back down the trail. Nobody would shoot him to beat him out of that prize, least of all Buckskin himself if that's what you were thinking, or that big fellow. I'll go out there right now and take a look around. Go tell Curley he's got a customer coming in. Get a box ready. I'm paying. Is Joe's body right on the trail where I can see it?"

"No," the rider said. "Behind a rock at the second bend."

"How'd you see him?"

"I had my dog out for a run and he turned him up."

"Where's the dog now?"

"I put him back on the chain, at the cabin, and then I came here quick as I could. Don't want him running loose after that killer. I need that dog for company. All I got these days."

"Dog act funny at all, with the body, the ground thereabouts?"

"I think he caught something on the air, Sheriff, the way he wanted to go looping about, but I wasn't about to poke around alone after a dead shot who got a bead on Deadshot Joe Collier. Shooter could be hiding behind a hundred rocks or trees."

"Go tell Curley, and tell Maxwell I'm looking for him. He's probably in The Sundowner."

As Wallace waited for his deputy, Carl Maxwell, he ran the marksmen through his mind, seeing the three mountain men as near triplets as possible, though they never hung out together. "Don't covet anyone's ground or traps," he thought, "the three of them saying so, like sworn obligations, and don't get too close to another human being, being another rule for true mountain men. They've spent most of their time up there as loners, free of this little chunk of civilization. Can't blame them for that."

Some of the gathered crowd of hill people read those words as a wish from the sheriff, mountain life hard enough in the beginning and all through it without being bushwhacked at the end.

The door of Wallace's office swung in and Buckskin, big as a mountain himself, edged his way through. "That right, what I heard about Joe, Sheriff? Bushwhacked?"

He sat down with a bit of disgust in his movement, shaking his head, a forlorn look on his face, a deep sigh escaping his chest. "Once in a while, up there," and he turned his head and looked off to the northern mountains, "I caught his smoke in the air. Smelt it or saw it, like company was around. Kind of trusty like.

106

I'll miss that. He favored our end of the mountain. That other new feller likes the other end, the big gent, the Newsome feller."

"No signs of anybody else up there?" Wallace said.

"Oh, week or so back," said Buckskin, "near the second falls coming off Big Ben, I saw some tracks, but they didn't wander far. I figure someone might have been looking at that old mine near the falls. Seen others a year back or so. Bodies playing games at getting rich, but ain't ever happening, to my mind. Place is as clean as new boots. There ain't a sparkle left in the whole mountain, like the ace of diamonds being the river card you're pulling for out of one lousy deck."

"Who'd want to cash in Joe?" Wallace said. "He didn't have anything but his rifles, his mules, his gear. Not much for a man to leave in this life."

"Oh, it ain't so bad up there, Phil. Being alone ain't the worst thing in the world. That crowd out there now makes me want to run back up there and have my fire, my coffee, and my thoughts. Ain't many people here in town can match the silence I know. When I saw a bit of smoke or smelled a slab of bear meat on a hot stick, I always figured Joe was kind of saying hello. Be lonely now, but if you're going out there to have a look see, then I'm bound to go with you." He nodded in self-agreement. "Like a family thing," he added.

"The shoot goes off an hour before sundown. I'll have you back by then, so's you can get your shots in."

"It ain't very important, Phil," Buckskin said, and the sheriff could sense him balancing out his values.

The sheriff, his deputy and Buckskin wandered through the area where Joe Collier's body was found. Neither of the lawmen noticed any kind of clue, the sheriff feeling they had to look anyway; perhaps a clue might fall into their laps. It sure wasn't going to come from the ground, he thought, shaking his head, lost, though knowing where he was.

But it was Buckskin, in a mess of rocks that had probably fallen in place a thousand or more years before, who raised his arms, then his voice. "Up here, Phil. Take a look see here." He pointed at his feet, where he was standing in the maze of rocks and two huge blow downs well into a rotting stage. The two trees had fallen, crossed each other, all limbs about gone, the trunks almost like old oatmeal.

"I'm looking, Buckskin, but I don't see anything that'd set me thinking. Better point it out to me. I'm getting too old to see the spots in front of my eyes."

"What I see is easy for an old mountain man, Phil. Right here, up against this old tree trunk a man with a rifle knelt himself down and pointed his rifle over the other trunk. He would have had an easy shot at anyone on the trail." He looked both ways and said, "Coming or going. And it looked like Joe got by before that bushwhacker rat pulled the trigger."

"It doesn't point out anybody to us, Buckskin. Could be anybody in town. Anybody come in for the shoot. Got Joe out of sight is all else he did, hiding his body."

"Told us one other thing," Buckskin said, "told us he was a lefty." He put his one knee into a depressed spot on the lower trunk and his other elbow on the crossing trunk.

"Like this," he said, assuming the pose of a bushwhacker, the scowl of hatred on his face. The pose was a natural for taking aim, shooting. With his face turned away from the sheriff's sight, Buckskin could have been anybody in Churchfree, anybody there all the time, anybody who come in for the shoot.

Sheriff Wallace said, "We'll have a look at any lefties that turn up, ask a few questions. 'Bout all we got."

Buckskin, smiling, said, "Well, we'll see, Phil. We'll see."

Wallace detected something in Buckskin's voice, but let it sit in the back of his mind.

The trio of searchers was back in Churchfree before the shoot was to get underway.

It was a scene in the village that late afternoon. The sun was sitting on the mountain tops, like a flash of fire on taller peaks, and rushes of sweet pink and pale green and summer orange shone down through the passes and the valleys forming mountain range connections. Bustle was afoot in the village, and ladies rushed with trays of goodies for the contestants and had long set to flames the carcasses brought to butchering.

In the squeezed-in hamlet, the children of miners and hill people, servicing travelers that had to climb the Rockies to get to the Pacific and San Francisco and other points, tossed their energies into the end of day and could be heard all over the mountain walls, the sounds bouncing, the glee contagious. Three short-haul stages were due in, one staying, two passing on. Denver Pacific Railroad men, working a dozen miles away, signaling the end of Churchfree within a few years, came in for

108

the shoot. The railroad, already to Denver a half dozen years earlier, was doing lots of maintenance work and had a large force of workers. The gaiety and anticipation and excitement built a common fever among all the inhabitants and visitors in the tight little village. Five minutes earlier the bar at the Sundowner Saloon was filled with men shoulder to shoulder, their voices rising, their bets being made and money held for prize winners. At the sound of a bell they all scrambled to get a viewing position or to get into the shooter's line to take their shots.

Buckskin, in line with all the other contestants, managed to get beside one lefty known to him, and the big feller, Newsome, from the other end of the mountain.

"Say, Newsome, any strange events happen around you on your way into Churchfree for the shoot?"

"Damned right there was, Buckskin. Either was a stray shot or a bad shot, because I felt or heard a slug come too damned close for the liking. But I didn't see anybody. If I had my dog with me, we'd have run him to ground. You thinking there's some connection with Joe Collier's getting counted like he was?"

Buckskin chimed in, "Right on. We found where the bushwhacker took a shot, over an old blow down." He looked from Newsome to the other lefty right beside him in the line. "We got a pretty good lead on who did it. Left his calling card all over the place."

"How you meaning that?" Newsome said.

"The rat was a lefty. Me and the sheriff saw that real easy. A lefty rat."

Newsome, irked, quizzical, said, "You ain't talking about me, are you, Buckskin? I'm a lefty."

Buckskin was ready for his deepest thrust. "No. We already checked you out, Newsome, and we know you didn't do it. The lefty who did it knelt on the old blow down and picked up some of the coloring from the rot. His knee would be messy brown by now."

The other lefty, looking down quickly at his own pant leg felt the gun in his back as the sheriff took away his rifle. "We're going to do some talking, mister, back at the jail. Me and Buckskin and this other big feller who's awful interested in things. If I was you I wouldn't think of running. These two gents could drop you half way down the mountain. And you ain't even gonna get a chance to take your shots in the contest after all of this. I call that even Steven stuff."

109

The sheriff said to Buckskin and Newsome. "You two fellers go win some prizes while I run this feller right to a comfortable jail cell. That's about all he's gonna win."

110

Doc Hannah's Honeymoon

The marriage of Beth Neville and Doc Hannah had taken place, guests and the balance of the wedding party had departed a few hours earlier from Doc's house outside Caliper, Texas, and night, darkness and ultimate romance fostered in the mix. Beth was in the bedroom changing for comfort and Doc Hannah was cleaning up a few odds and ends left over in the kitchen. The clatter at the porch threw everything out of kilter and the door was thrown wide open.

Two men, with drawn guns, entered the house, supporting between them a man who was wounded and bleeding. He was hatless, without gun belt or weapon in sight, and his eyes were caught up by an inner pain that showed on his face in steady grimaces.

"You got a customer, Doc," one man said, as they dropped their wounded companion onto a couch. The speaker was a huge, brawny man in a colored calico shirt, a neckerchief knotted in place, and a bowler on his head rather than a sombrero that most cowboys in the area wore.

The big man spoke again. "He caught a bullet in his gut down range, Doc. You got a few hours to get him fixed up."

Doc Hannah did not know any of the men.

It was not Doc Hannah's first experience with a wounded bad guy brought to his door by saddle pards. It had been only six months or so since Bad Boy Ben Hooter had come in the door in the dead of night, crying, his kid brother slung over his shoulder.

Now, on this new occasion, Hannah did not look at the bedroom door, diverting the men by asking, in a brisk and important manner, "How long ago was he shot? Tell me the exact time. I have to know." He grabbed his traveling bag from beside the door and knelt beside the new patient. The man's shirt front was covered with blood, turning dark red from exposure.

Doc Hannah, keeping their attention on himself, was collecting information so he could pinpoint the hour of the crime, and the possible location, based on travel lore. At the same time he was hoping Beth would climb out the window and get away before one of the men found her. He could not remember if he had told Beth he kept a gun in every room, just in case. Here, in this room, the lone revolver was tucked into the couch on which the wounded man now rested, his moans breaking loose with each cough, as if a sucking chest wound was making headway on him.

111

The sounds were ominous.

"We came to you, Doc, because we heard down the trail you lived out here alone, not liking town life. We're pure glad of that. I hope you got nobody comin' out this way tonight, Doc. No late date or somethin' like that. One of the ladies from town or from one of the ranches. You're a good lookin' doggie, Doc. But we don't need no other company. You just get our boy Jed here all fixed up and we'll be on our way. Best do a good job, Doc. He won't like it none at all if you don't do it up good. He had a bad temper before all this happened. No tell where it's gone with him since then. I bet he's meaner than a stuck peccary, it don't go his way." He assessed what he had said; "Me neither, Doc. Me neither."

Beth, in the bedroom, had heard it all. Every word. In her slippered feet, she had put on a pair of denim dungarees and a sweater. Her dress and other wedding togs had been put away earlier, in the back of a chest; she'd not be wearing them again, she hoped. Even as she kept telling herself not to make a single sound, she studied the window. She'd have get out and do one of two things: go for help or find some way to divert the attention of the men so that her new husband could make a quick and safe escape. The outside of the house came into focus in her mind as she remembered how far the windows sat above ground level. This one, beside her, Beth hoped, was the same as the others, not far from the ground level.

The mirror on the bureau she noticed again, the one that Doc had purchased for her from a furniture drummer as one of her wedding presents, was bigger than the mirror in her bedroom back home on the ranch.

Looking into it, Beth saw a new bride who had been waiting for her new husband. Then, in a flash, she saw a girl still in her teens who was in a crisis. Staring at herself, looking into her eyes, she saw her mother's bright blue eyes looking back at her. The nod on both sides of the glass was slow and deliberate.

She stepped to the window and, in a cursory sweep of her head, saw the butt of a rifle behind the mirror. The ball of breath, caught in her chest, she feared could be heard in the other room. There was the butt of a familiar Springfield Trapdoor Rifle, model 1873, the kind of weapon she was familiar with from using it for a few years on the ranch. It sat right behind the mirror on the back edge of the bureau. There was not much time, she decided, and looked at how she could get it free without making any noise. The

112

assumption came to her that the rifle had to be loaded, ready to fire. With great ease and steady hands, Beth slid the rifle along the rim of the bureau, holding her breath and holding the butt firmly in her hands. The weapon slid cleanly along the bureau, making no sound.

When she had the rifle in both hands, Beth leaned it against the wall beside the window, placing the gun sight into a fissure in the wall so the rifle would not slip. The major test would be to get the window open as quickly and as quietly as possible. There was one latch on the window, and only a stick to hold the whole window open from the bottom at a slant in warm weather. The latch opened silently and agile Beth placed the notched stick against the window frame and pushed the window open, careful to prevent the stick from slipping, making a noise, drawing the unexpected visitors into the room.

Doc Hannah's voice rose sharply from the other room, as if he was again trying to draw attention to his own person. "Dammit, man, will you hold his head up so he won't choke on his own spittle. He needs air."

"Don't get me goin', Doc, I don't need none of this. I don't want to be in your shoes he dies on us tonight. And I don't like none you gettin' so fidgety, like someone's comin' to see you tonight. I sure don't want none of those surprises."

"I don't give a damn what you're afraid of, mister. I'm just worried about me and my patient, that's all. Cut and dried, me and him. You don't count for me."

Another voice, so far unheard, said, "Why'n'cha knock him on the head, Trooper? We ought to beat it out of here soon. If he ain't goin' to get him fixed, make him tell us now. I think he knows what's comin' to Hank. He knows already, I bet. Doc's know things we never know, like right now."

Beth at that moment leaned out the window and placed the rifle outside, tipping it against the house. If she made a noise she didn't want them to see the rifle if they came rushing into the bedroom.

With one leg out the window, and holding the window with one hand, Beth lifted the stick and laid it down against the outside of the house beside the rifle. Then she lowered the window until it touched the crown of her head, drew her other leg over the windowsill and climbed out. When she lowered the window into place, only a single squeak was heard.

The heavy voice, reaching Beth outside, said, "What the hell are you smilin' at, Doc? Paulie, go check and make sure nobody's hidin' in there. I swear I heard somethin'."

A door squeaked. Paulie, the third man, said, "Nobody in here, Trooper. Looks like he was gettin' ready for sleep."

Doc Hannah, pleased and surprised, had a series of images run through his head. He envisioned Beth slipping out the window and moving slowly to the barn and going out the side door of the small barn with her horse, but without saddle, without reins, and without being frantic. He had married one special lady, and he loved her dearly, but he hoped she was about to break and run for it. That horse of hers could make it to town quicker than the bad guys could.

No sound of hoof beats came to him. No musical gallop. Nothing.

"Doc," Trooper said, his voice angry, louder, "What the hell's happenin' now? Hank looks like he's plain dyin' on us." The wounded man was caught up in a spasm of sound and bodily commotion. "You better not let him die, Doc. Him and his brother won't like it very much."

"None of them count much now," Doc Hannah said, as he knew the wounded man had taken his last serious breath in life.

The gasp was audible in all corners of the room.

"That's it, Doc," Trooper said, "you did a lousy job. I ought to finish you now."

Doc Hannah ducked as the window exploded and a round tore into the gun arm of Trooper, the hand on that arm not quite reaching his pistol.

"What the hell is that?" Paulie exclaimed, as he too ducked out of sight beside the couch, and Doc Hannah, physician, range boy for all his growing years, dove for the revolver hidden in the couch. He leveled it at Paulie, sitting on the floor, shaking his head, unsure of what had happened. Not until Hannah had pulled Paulie's weapons from their holsters, and trained them on him, did Paulie realize what happened as Beth came rushing in the door and hugged her new husband, still in one piece.

The doc hugged her back.

"This is where I belong," she said, not caring who heard her, not caring how long it would be before someone came from town to check on how their night had gone, and her doctor having another patient on his hands.

114

Doc Hannah's Replacement

Caliper, Texas poured just about every citizen out for the goodbye to Doc Hannah and his wife Beth as they were bidding goodbye to the pair, off for a new location in west Texas. With two boys in tow the pair was bound for Clinton after Doc had arranged for Toby Maxwell, his assistant for two years, to be his replacement in Caliper. The gala was attended by the whole town of Caliper, saying goodbye to the good doctor who had served them for almost ten years. The doc was a beloved individual whose work had touched practically every person in the town.

Toby Maxwell, blond and excitedly good looking according to some of his younger female patients, reveled in his new assignment, believing he had learned just about all the ropes that Doc Hannah could twirl. That included the business of doctoring and the business of people. Ever on, he remembered what Hannah had said about being a doctor in a small western town: "Don't close your eyes to anything that's worth seeing, Toby. Keep it all with you. It may help in decision-making somewhere down the trail, down-range." Ten years as a horse and buggy doctor gave serious credence to anything Doc Hannah ever offered to a listener.

Toby Maxwell was a listener.

Shorter than Hannah, smaller in his frame, but sporting a blaze of red hair, Maxwell had made a notable start in Caliper after finishing school in the East. His arrival in Caliper was a memorable if not enviable occasion. When he alighted from the Caliper-Fremont stage, two robbers bolted from the Caliper Bank with a bundle of cash and took Maxwell as a hostage. He was gone for five days before the sheriff and one of his deputies found him wandering alone in the foothills of the Morgan Mountain Range. For a newcomer, he had quickly become saddle-broken, trail-wise, and able to handle a hot skillet over an open fire, all under direction of a revolver waved at him by one of the bank robbers.

He quickly understood some of the gestures. "I know what you mean most of the time, the way you point that gun," he'd said on occasion, but always adding, "you still can't be too careful waving a gun around. Just ask me how many 'accidents' doctors have treated. There have been awful accidents where none of them could do a thing for the injured party; not when they turn out deadly. I hope I don't have a turn at treating any of you gents."

115

Once again, before any of them could reply, he wondered what Doc Hannah would do in this situation, as the Doc's reputation had "gone east" after many incidents.

"I hope that's not a threat, Doc," one of the men said. The others called him "Z." Maxwell figured "Z" was the boss. He'd keep his eye on that man, he vowed softly, and thought of Doc Hannah again and what he had written in the letter that stated the new need for a doctor in Caliper. The words had stuck in his mind.

"Use your brain," came to him in internal translation, "Don't be timid. Doctors can't be timid. Doctors take chances. We doctors must find ways not yet in our hands." Strange as it seemed, the internal voice seemed, at every syllable, to be Doc Hannah's voice, though he had never written the words that Maxwell was sure he heard. "As a doctor, you may be the last stand, the final great barrier between you and quick death for untold people. Be ready, Toby. Be ready."

The letter was in Maxwell's pocket, creased a dozen times, re-read a dozen times.

With these thoughts working in the gray matter, three times Maxwell tried to escape, two times recaptured, two times punished.

When they caught up to him the first time, they beat him up pretty badly. But Doc Maxwell did not punch back, not wanting to hurt his hands. "I'm no surgeon," he readily admitted to himself, "but I have to take care of these hands." He was, of course, talking about ministering to all those patients on his western horizon. "Down range," he might have said, "or somewhere along the trail." It was all said out there in his future, if there was going to be a future. He'd have to do his best to get away; "The West," people kept saying, "was wide open."

One of his captors, called Bucko, said to his padres after the first escape attempt, as if admonishing them, "Let's treat the doc better next time. We might need him."

The next day was the next time. Maxwell jumped on a horse, but it was hobbled and went nowhere. Bucko said, "You got spirit and gumption, Doc, but damned foolish, if you ask me. Nobody jumps on a horse still hobbled. Can hurt the damned animal if you think about it."

Then he turned to Maxwell, jabbed him on the shoulder and said, "Doc, if we ever git into a runnin' gun fight, make damned sure you keep your head down. We gotta keep you lucky long as we can. If the Big Man gets a new job for us, you might come in handy. Never can tell who's a better shot than the last guy. Some of 'em couldn't hit a barn door if they was standin' on it and pointin' down."

Maxwell figured "Z" and the "Big Man" were not one and the same, but he kept his eyes on Bucko from the first moment he had seen him fall asleep as soon as he dismounted from his horse in a wooded section. That's when he remembered hearing about a French doctor named Gelineau who studied people who fell asleep easily. Gelineau called the disorder "narcolepsy," having derived its name from two Greek words, "narko" meaning numbness, and "lepsis" meaning attack. This was not the first time Maxwell had seen a case of the sickness.

The young doctor put that information in a corner of his mind. He hoped the situation to use it would arise.

In the meantime, Doc Hannah and his wife Beth decided they could not leave Caliper with the new doctor's life at risk. They truly didn't know if they'd ever see him again. Beth told her friends that Doc Hannah thought Toby Maxwell would become one of the west's truly fine doctors. "Doc says that he knows Toby has come in contact with newer medicine developments and various treatments. So, he'll be a great medical addition to the town. And you better treat him right if and when he gets back here. Doc's convinced it will take a great deal to hold Toby down. He's heard a lot about him from folks he trusts. Let's hope he's right."

Eventually the grimy robbers, about 50 miles away in the foothills, took time to have a swim in the heat of the day. Bucko was assigned to keep his eye on Maxwell, but he fell asleep in the middle of a yawn. With the other two bank robbers in the middle of a washing swim, Maxwell simply rode away, riding one horse and driving off all the other mounts with the loudest yells he could muster. In turn, he was shot at, ducked, rode hard, and made his way over a hill and down into a series of canyons. Finally, after being lost for a whole day, Sheriff Slade Burton and a deputy, coming from a town down in the lower territory, found him sitting beside the road, his horse halted by a limp.

Maxwell told them where he had been.

Sheriff Burton said, "We heard all about your problem with them bank robbers, Doc. A couple of freighters told us on the trail. Where'd you leave them robbers takin' their yearly bath? Stream water or pond water?"

"They were in a small stream, Sheriff, getting rid of half a year of crud."

Maxwell was trying to remember all he had seen, but so much of the land had appeared for him in such a short and tenuous time. "The water came right off a small waterfall. A drop of no more than 20 feet. Lots of trees around the place, so no one could see us from the trail. I had no idea where I was, but when I got on the horse, I blazed out of there. I heard them talking a few times, saying they couldn't afford to let me go because I'd know them any place, especially in court, after spending a few days waiting on them." He shook his head in exasperation. "It was like I graduated from cooking school instead of medical school."

Burton laughed, but not too heavily. He had decided he admired the redheaded doctor in a quick assessment. "That'd be on Elm Hill Creek, Doc," he said, "where there's a small waterfall I saw once or twice. A dozen or more mile from here, and back up that way." He tossed his head half-heartedly in a northerly direction, as if signifying it was too late or of no use starting out at this time.

"It's best we go back now," he said in qualification. "We'll look at a few posters, if you don't mind, Doc. Sounds like it's the Main Street Gang from Independence. Pretty active this side of the big river, but if they stay this side, they'll show up somewhere along the line. We'll have to look at the posters. If it ain't them, we'll get Curly Somers the drawer to draw up some more and let you do the decidin' on their looks."

A second thought came to Burton. "You catch any of their names, Doc?"

"'Z,' Big Man and Bucko were all I heard for names, like they might have been covering up, but that's kind of ridiculous because they knew I could and would identify each one if given the chance later on."

"That tells me, Doc, they wasn't about to let you go less'n you hotfooted out of there like you did. That was darn good on your part, Doc. Doc Hannah would say so hisself. But none of those names mean anythin' to me, includin' what I know of the Main Street Gang.

They were just about to mount up when the sheriff said, "Doc, you notice any brands on their horses? Any marks to set them off? Might say somethin' else about them, if you was to remember anythin' like that."

"Well, Sheriff, that's funny you should ask me that," Maxwell said. "They changed horses one time way off in some canyon, from another guy who kept himself out of my site. But one of the new horses had a mark like a small arrow wearing a circle. I didn't see anything on the other horses."

Burton, winking slyly at his deputy and pursing his lips just as slyly, said "Why, thanks a lot, Doc. That's some kind of help. On the way back to Caliper, we're goin' over to Ridley for a quick visit. Yes, siree, Doc Hannah's got hisself a real good replacement. He'd say you'll do, Doc. Yes, sir. Nothin' like Doc Hannah's cure for the trouble that ails you."

The deputy's mouth still hung open as they mounted, the sheriff nodding "No" with his head or "Keep your mouth shut."

He believed Maxwell was oblivious of his signals.

Four lazy hours later, Maxwell faring well in the saddle as if he was born on a ranch, the trio approached Ridley. Burton spoke at length to Maxwell in a huddle, and then he and his deputy rode into town ahead of Maxwell, who followed a few minutes later and rode slowly and unobtrusively down the main street and rode down between the Prairie Dog Saloon and the general store.

The sheriff and his deputy rode directly to the Ridley sheriff's office.

But Toby Maxwell had his own ideas.

Burton, on entering the sheriff's office, said to the big man standing beside his desk, "Carl Ruskin, it's been a couple of years since I ran into you. You ain't much older."

"Hell, Slade," the Ridley sheriff said, "If I chased you on my best horse, I couldn't catch up to all those years you got pilin' up. But I can say, you're wearin' well as could be supposed. What trots you all the ways up here?"

He looked at the young deputy and said, "You look dry as turds, son. I'll git you a beer at the saloon in a few minutes, seein' as the boss there hasn't let you wet your whistle yet."

Slade Burton, sitting wearily on a straight-back chair, rubbed his sleeve on his badge and said huskily, as if to set the tone for his visit, "We're here after a local, Carl, for kidnappin' our new doctor and robbin' our bank. We found the doc wanderin' on the trail after near a week off with the robbers, one of them sportin' a Circle Arrow brand. Man might be a horse thief or workin' off the spread. If he's at the saloon or comes in, the doc will be in town later on and we can grab him, maybe without firin' a shot, which would be my choice."

119

"I'm with you there, Slade. The quieter the better for old folks such as us."

All that wishful thinking was about to fly the coop as Doc Maxwell rode directly into the livery after looking at the half dozen horses tied up at the saloon hitch rail.

"Good day, sir," Maxwell said to the livery man. "My name's Toby Maxwell. I'm Doc Hannah's replacement at Caliper, and I need a gun. Can you loan me one?"

"Well, Doc, I done heard about you. All us here at Ridley been talkin' 'bout it for near a week. Is this getting' even time for you?" Visible to him was a fire starting up in Maxwell's eyes, and his cheeks showing some real color in a quick change.

"Yes, it is," Maxwell said, "and the man who kidnapped me and kept me waitin' on him and his bunch is pretty sure to be in the saloon right now. I saw a horse I've seen before. I want to see the look on this gent's face when a gun's in my hand. I figure it's part of my western learning. Can you help me out, like a good neighbor?"

"My pleasure, Doc. I got me a Colt revolver will make a man say ouch in a hurry. It's all yours. And I know where that horse comes from, the one you're ridin.'"

"Stolen?"

"Permanen'ly, as some might say," he mumbled, as if aware of his speech pattern, "or for holdin' on, 'cause it was stole from me right here 'bout two weeks ago, when I was at the saloon havin' my supper one evenin'."

"You have your horse back," Maxwell said, "and," as if to balance an equation, added, "I'll borrow your Colt."

"Evens goin' Stevens fits me good, Doc. It shoots a little high," the livery man said as he handed Maxwell the Colt. "You'll have to stick it in your belt. I ain't got no holster for it. Be careful of them guys who steal horses, rob banks, take doctors for hostagin'. They don't care for nothin', seems."

"Being as mad as I've ever been doesn't make this easy for me. Not even being made a fool of. I just like to see Old Lady Justice get the line toed and in order, and the bad guys properly put in place."

With the Colt stuck under his belt, Doc Maxwell headed for the saloon. The red was on his face and in his eyes, as if the long-dormant fire had found ignition. Dust rose under his stomping feet from the one road in town. Like an avenging angel he strode, with the gun suddenly in his hand. An old-timer jumped into the sheriff's office.

Doc Maxwell slammed open the door of the saloon as if he was a marshal on an arrest. In one glance he saw two of the robbers, two of his kidnappers. Bucko was asleep, hanging over a table. The other, still nameless in Maxwell's mind, went to draw his gun, but the new doctor had a Colt aimed at his face.

"I have all the right in the world to kill you right now, but I suspect the sheriff is on his way here right now. Maybe I'll wait for him and maybe I won't." The Colt was as steady in his hand as if it was a scalpel descending for the initial cut.

Bucko woke up, fishing his eyes around for clarity, trying to see what he thought he was seeing; the doc standing there with a gun on his pard. Something in the doc's face said, "Don't play with me now. I've got the drop on you roustabouts."

Bucko knew the doc had a lot of guts. Flat on the table he placed his hands, just as the two sheriffs and a deputy entered the saloon, guns drawn.

Immediately all the people in the saloon were measuring things: the bad guys looking at the drawn guns; Sheriff Burton, all the way from Caliper, studied Maxwell from stem to stern; the Ridley sheriff watched the bad guys still sitting at a table; the owner of the saloon looked at the third mirror behind the bar in less than two years; and Doc Maxwell, counting his five days as a working hostage, felt something leaving him, like a phantom was losing ground.

Slade Burton, waving his gun, said, "Hold it there, Doc. Don't let the last five days take care of forever. Doc Hannah still needs you in Caliper. Hell, all of us need you, so you drop that weapon and we'll get on with takin' care of them five days for you, best we can.

The old livery man, standing at the door of the saloon, was heard to say, "This here's sure a right sight, Evens Stevens gettin' done. And the doc's right again."

121

The Barber of Copa Verdi

Just after the break of dawn, a cool September morning, Stem Swensen rode into Copa Verdi with a near empty saddle bag, a rifle without ammo, and no change of clothes. He looked the part he announced, or announced the part he looked... on the skids, on the run, on the take if he could find an angel with gifts. Even with all that, some people of the town took notice when he entered Paulie's Tonsorial Palace. His beard was, without doubt, a month's worth of bush.

Paulie in the barbershop, as disillusioned as a man could get, said, "You can shave yourself, mister, 'cause I'm cutting outta here before the day is out. There's plenty of hot water over there in that kettle, and what's left of the soap and cream is yours for the taking. I have shaved my last beard, trimmed my last head of wrangler's hair, and soaked the last sot back to sobriety or propriety, however you'll have it. The sheriff can bang on the door all he wants."

He watched with glee as Swenson soaked his face, lathered his beard, took a razor from his shirt pocket, and cleaned his face of hair as swift and as smooth as ever seen. He saw, in the difference, a whole personality change.

"You belong in a place like this, mister, carrying your own blade and working it like that. You can have the place for $25, payment due the first of the month after the next month. Time enough for raising the investment. I'll be over in La Petra working for my old boss, Trip Eggerman. He has his hand on the pulse of the whole territory, and thinks something good is going to happen around here."

"Like what?" Swenson said, interest riding on his new face, expressions more easily read.

Paulie brought up a half smile on his own face. "Private stuff comes with the job. You come in here, work the place, play dumb, keep your ears open and I'll guarantee you'll catch some stuff worth gold if used right. Don't be too hungry, don't push too hard or too fast and it'll fall right into your apron."

He dropped a black linen apron into Swenson's hands. "Don't take too long thinking about it. 'Nother gent said he might be interested, but he won't be back off the posse until tomorrow at the earliest. I heard from Eggerman they're way over Tascosa way chasing a couple of robbers hit the stage a week or so ago. Black Cat Pownel's one of them, and they say he come across

122

the Big Lady Mississippi for the first time ever, looking for a piece of the bank for hisself, after raising hell in Tennessee. "

Swenson, showing adventure or a new kind of gambling at hand, said, "All I need is a grubstake for the first day on the job. Maybe enough for a meal and a beer. He reached into his saddlebag and held up a small, dark, metallic-looking object. "This here's a souvenir from a real New York bank a gent gave me when I got him out from under his rolled and dead horse. It's worth some kind of stake for a steak." He smiled.

Paulie, picking up on a slice of humor, said, "And a few beans and a beer. Okay by me," and handed Swenson a gold dollar piece. "The deal is done. You're the new barber of Copa Verdi." The object sat in his hands. "What is it?"

"It's just a trinket, a souvenir from a bank for making deposits, but it's real silver. He said it fell off a wagon right there in front of him in Philadelphia as he was coming this way, in a hurry, of course. His horse, when I come up on them, had two broken legs and I had to knock him out of this life before I pulled the gent loose."

Paulie smiled his understanding. "Did that lucky, finally undid gent happen to rob that there bank in Philadelphia? That's some kind of story. Keep telling them like that and you'll get yourself some steady hair customers. But put your good efforts at great shaves. Great shaves get remembered, the kind that brings a fellow back from where he's gone in sour times. There's always sour times hanging around. "

The real world suddenly sat full on Paulie's face when he offered a weighty piece of advice as if he was dredging it out of his mind like he'd once read it in a big book, passing on the minor legacy of the barber shop. "Best other thing I can tell you is keep a gun close to hand. Like under a loose shirt or hung by the soap mugs or right in your holster, but the holster show makes you one of them whose hair you're cutting or shaving their necks and that gets them real uncomfortable. One time comes you need a gun, better have it close. Temper changes men considerably, and there's a lot of things happening around here. Some gents are going to have good luck and some are going to have bad luck. Watch for the difference 'cause they'll all come by here once a month or better and most'll carry their disposition like a sign hung right out there on their chests. That should get you to know a man pretty good. It's hardly any different than following trail. All you got to do is read the signs."

He finished up with another piece of advice. "Best spend your new-gotten money, at least for starting, over at the hotel. Best food in town. Miss Jackson Melba Abilene's one great cook and one great lady. She don't play any games with you or your money. If you want a friend in town, trust her. She is real trustable." Paulie walked out on his five-year investment, and Stem Swenson had his first customer before he could get to spend any of his small stake.

"I just saw Paulie headin' for the livery. Says he's done with barberin' and shavin' and that you gotta pretty steady hand. I'm needing a fix-up. Name's John Weller and I don't like no gun at your side when you got me all hunkered up." He sat in the big chair and saw his face in the mirror. "Best get home cleaner than this. Woman 'spects to recognize me out by the gate. And I been gone on trail for a spell." Then, to cap off his homecoming, he added, "Throw on some of that pretty stuff Paulie says can't do no harm at all." His hand was on his own revolver until Swenson tossed his up on the little shelf where the pretty stuff was.

Swenson said, "I'm not anywhere as good with the gun as I am with this razor. I brought it along the trail with me all the way from Philadelphia my last trip home. Got another one just like it in my saddle bag."

Weller sparked with interest. "I guess you're figurin' on stayin'. You ever see the Liberty Bell?"

"I sure did, but it wasn't in Philadelphia. I saw it on a train in Maryland one day when I was heading out from home. They had it out for traveling around some of the country."

"Didn't hear it ring? That would've sprung me all loose, for a whole day anyhow, just thinking about it."

"I didn't hear it ring. Don't think it rung at all, not down there in Maryland. Heard it had a crack made it dumb." Swenson nodded his head in a mark of frustration and swung the conversation around in full stride. "That Paulie who sold me this place thinks this area's going to get good things happening to it. You think that's true?"

"Hell, no. I just heard Black Cat Pownel's scouting out the area this side of the big river, wanting a new home, a new hang-out, getting' chased outta too many places from what I hear. Sheriff got no call on him here but rumors sail fast as tumbleweed front of a fire. There's some say he's already got a new gang. Any strangers come in here for shaving and such, don't wear that gun on the hip." He nodded at Swenson's gun sitting on the shelf. "It

124

don't say welcome." He sat back in the chair as Swenson swung a hot towel over his beard, leaving his first customer's eyes clear so he could see in the big mirror who was coming or going, or even passing by with so much as a hint of looking in. The same precautions held true at a campfire out on the trail; both men in the shop knowing survival anywhere demanded alertness, awareness at all times, good lines of sight.

"From what I heard myself, coming past the Mississippi, is all that stuff about Black Cat is all made up. Nobody's ever seen him rob a bank or a train, nor shoot that lady in the stagecoach that was sitting near the bank in Missouri one time."

"I never heard about that one, not about no lady gettin' shot up while she was sittin' still, maybe waitin' to go someplace special for her or just gettin' there. Sure is a damned shame, that twist of the Black Cat."

"See, pard, that's what I mean," Swenson said as he started the heavy lathering. "Some gent sitting here listening to me might walk out of here and start saying that stuff all over the place. Pretty soon this Black Cat gent is hung for nothing he did."

"You talk like you was favorin' him. I bet I'd watch my tongue I was you. That Black Cat's got lots of meanness goin' for him right now, and most people won't let it go."

"I guess you'd be one of them," Swenson said, sliding that smooth edge down over Weller's chin, Weller sitting real still at the move. "I don't crib my words at all, John Weller. I wouldn't go to your hanging either less they proved to me you did some crime and someone truthful saw it and swore it. Same way with the Black Cat, or whatever they call him for real. I don't want to see no man hang for something he might have done." Swenson drew the next pass of the razor down over Weller's face. The razor made no sound at all and Weller smiled and closed his eyes.

"You got some kind of smooth, mister. Never felt a second of that."

Swenson knew for a fact that the smooth draw down on Weller's face would be echoed in the saloon before nightfall. As well as his stand on trials and juries and hangings, and the Black Cat in particular.

Three weeks later, Swenson by then a piece of town fabric and his trade prospering, the Black Cat still a matter of talk, the sheriff and a small posse were chasing down some rustlers a ways out of town. At the peak of noon on an idle Saturday, four men walked into the bank, drew bandanas or kerchiefs over their faces,

125

showed their guns in earnest fashion and ordered saddle bags to be filled with new paper money.

"We don't want all of it," one big robber said, "just most of it."

When they left, the last man going out the door tossed a wood carving of a black cat at the feet of the teller. It was painted a glossy black. The man, his kerchief still tight in place, said, "Tell the sheriff I said hello." He pointed at the carving at the teller's feet and offered a conciliatory nod the teller understood all the way.

The robbers made off with a good haul, and the word went all over the territory that the Black Cat had struck again.

Stem Swenson was in a number of arguments with customers, the barkeep at the saloon, and the sheriff himself. "How do you know, sheriff, it was Black Cat Pownel that did it?" Who saw him? Nobody according to the teller. Who's to say it was the Black Cat?"

"Hell, man, he left his calling card. That carved kitty. That's his sign."

"Who says so?" Swenson said. "I never heard any talk like that on the other side of the river. Nobody ever said anything about a carved toy."

"You sticking up for him, Mr. Barber?" The sheriff's tone was getting stiff and edgy. "Sounds odd to me, the stand you take."

"You like to see a man hung for something he didn't do? Is that a piece of your law here, sheriff? Is the Black Cat wanted here?"

"He is now."

"Was he wanted here before this robbery?"

"No, he wasn't."

At the other end of the bar, John Weller broke himself loose from some trail hands getting wet and joined the sheriff and Stem Swenson. "Sheriff," he said, "you make damn sure you don't put the barber on the jury when you catch the Black Cat. He'll give him the key and let him walk away he has the chance."

Swenson, putting himself apart from the sheriff leaning on the bar, said, "Do you know where John Weller was during the robbery, sheriff? You know where Artie here behind the bar was? Or Crokie over there and his pal, Thurman? Or me, for that matter?"

"Course I do," the sheriff said, "I got my trails all covered, considering the robbers were all masked up. Weller was with me. Artie here was setting them up right where he is now. Crokie and Thurman were on the drive with Eggerman. And you, Mr. Barber, were working in the barbershop. You had a big day, from what I heard. You made some headway in that place already, but you're falling short as an upstanding citizen, from where I see it. If you're putting people in places where they weren't, to explain yourself and your take on things, and throw dirt on my fire at the same time, it won't cut it with me."

Swenson had his palms up, a prelude to his questions. "You have a poster on Black Cat, sheriff? A drawing or picture of him? How will you know him to arrest him?"

The sheriff smiled again, a coy smile. "If we catch him in the act, or with some of them cat carvings, we got our man. It's that easy."

"Is that enough for you to put a rope around a man's neck? You feel sure about that, without seeing him do what a plain old somebody said he did?"

"You sound like a damned lawyer, Mr. Barber."

"What if those carved kitties were in your place if we searched it tonight?"

"But you all know me. I'm the sheriff. You know I won't do something like that."

"Won't or wouldn't or didn't?" Swenson leaned on the last part. "There's a whole lot of difference if the rope's dropping around your neck, wouldn't you say so, sheriff? Won't or wouldn't or didn't? Which one would you lean on first?"

The sheriff was visibly uneasy for the first time. "You got a ton of questions for a barber new in town. Don't seem natural. Why's that?"

John Weller, suddenly taller than he'd been in a week, said, "I told you there was something fishy about the new barber. He's too damn smooth for just a barber."

"My real name is Ed Pownel," Swenson said. "They call me The Black Cat, and I work for the railroad. I got a paper here from the governor, saying I'm checking out this area for a new line, but we're doing some other things for the governor at the same time, trying to find out the real lay of the land. What the law is like if things get busy here. Who's ready for big changes." He paused for a moment, and then added, "and who isn't." He carried

127

no expression on his face, but Weller and the sheriff did, looking oddly at each other.

Exodus Two, Western Style

In the coming morning Bartlett "Bart" Beauvais knew his oxen Reynard and Briscoe would stand as a pair like mountains on their own, their golden hides tossing early sun every which way toward noon, the shadows cast by their gigantic forms flattening on the earth as huge as continental maps fully laid out. Hungers of all kinds were being satisfied, was the way he made himself think.

But now, on his late watch, he searched for the new manner of signal, a totally new kind of signal. The whole story had come to him on the sly; that Kurgeth Kate and two of the girls from "upstairs in the Lake Paradise Saloon" had skipped town; out on their own in the hills, the mountains, the odd trails. A strange place for three ladies from Ambler's Grove, the lone, three-building town near Lake Paradise, a quick-start settlement not yet two years old.

"Skinned" Turcotte, once scalped by a lone brave and able to talk about it, which of course was his favorite pastime, had slipped to Beauvais' side in town that day and said, "I've a tidbit for you, Bart. A good one. I owe you from way back. Them three girls are in the hills, but don't walk in on them without warnin'. They're dead shots, each of them. I've seen 'em shoot the wings off'n birds, the ears of'n a baby bunny when Kate says she was just provin' a point to me. I know she told me 'cause she wanted me to tell you 'cause you was always good to her. She called you the best gent around. I hope I got some 'owesie' with you." He tipped his old hat from a scarred and a scary-looking scalp. "She's dead-set gettin' her first shot at the Big German, Louie Blusten, behind all the pain and misery and wantin' everythin' in sight."

Skinned proceeded to tell him the details of the warning, the social invite that might follow. It certainly perked Beauvais' interest. It had been said by many that Bartlett "Bart" Beauvais, farmer, ploughman, squatter, team driver, iron master, earth custodian, always kept a close eye on his pair of oxen. The man, it had been said a hundred times and more, made few friends, but kept those he made.

But he swore to his last days that he loved the golden pair Reynard and Briscoe best not only for their enormous strength, but for their endless on-ahead determination at huge and sometimes imponderable tasks. The stolid pair had taken him

129

west over the toughest terrain and through some close disasters. He could not recount the number of times they had surmounted a hill to get him into a good defensive position and out of danger. You can't say too much about friends like that.

Always moving someplace, he'd come out of Virginia and Maryland and admired the local strains of wood in those northeastern forests and all the useful applications they ended up in. With glee and deep satisfaction he had seen formidable oak used to form the ribs and keels of the huge sailing ships that plied the Atlantic, being no finer testament to northeast hardwoods, and also observed the different kinds of pines that shipbuilders used for masts of ships and ships' decking. In fact, as Beauvais moved west he carried and dutifully employed his precious portable mill to cut and hew all the usable trees en route for house and barn building on hire. His keen specialty was making the canvas-covered prairie schooners, those wagons that "constantly moved the east onto the west," all as commissioned along the way. Excitement, it was easy to see, came to him on every day at his passion, at his craft.

His few close friends would often close down talk of him by saying, "I swear the man can see the whole west explode in the back of his head." They knew it was his excitement of the American ideal and the American dream. Such movements move with such men, are carried on in a relentless manner. And always waking up the land that they pass through.   Of course, in time, he'd want to see Kurgeth Kate. Blonde, Nordic, part Swede and part Finn, she was about the most beautiful woman he'd ever seen. "We're naturals together," she'd offered more than once, her eyes gone over to a tint of pale green he'd never seen before. "And those eyes of yours, he offered in several replies, "Are as good as venison and Irish taters done in the fire." Privately, he agreed, those green eyes of hers, he'd swear on any book, glowed in the dark so he'd always know where she was.

He was, of course, an alert man. With visions coming as part of his make-up, Bart Beauvais knew history flourished around him, that he was in the middle of the mix where history was concerned, that no matter how small that new part appeared, it exerted impact. "Three girls leaving town, on their own, alert me, make me stick my chest out with pride at their making new stand on their own, in a place of their own choosing." Continually, as Beauvais moved, as he talked with old timers encountered on the trail, and the drovers and freighters and land planters and

130

ordinary hustlers met each day, he gathered what information he could on trees and what was happening in the territory. Trees, the near-science study he made of what he could accumulate, astounded him the way they generated new life by root, limb and leaf and air-borne seed spread, all which was added to his listing of trees and their best uses as firewood and building lumber and as special-adaptation wood. Capturing his attention, were the hundreds of trees that found their first grasp on the sides of sheer mountains, life starting on the sheer edge of life. On cliff edges, brief crevices, niches avoided for centuries, sepulchers of new growth.

His notes, because of his intense interest, grew prodigiously. When he arrived in Colorado and considered all the lumber lore he had gathered at the seaside on top of all he had absorbed about the various species like blue spruce, black walnut, black cherry, oak, gum, maple, soft yellow pine, yellow poplar, bristlecone pine, Douglas fir, lodge-pole pine, narrow-leaf cottonwood, aspen, birch, poplar, pinion pine, ponderosa pine. He considered himself a most highly educated man, a specialist without a degree that would ordinarily be made of one of the trees he loved.

Beauvais carried, on his trip west, a small, portable sawmill that could be run off water power or ox power. He'd worked in two such mills in West Virginia and knew about wood and the quality of trees; he knew the best grains, the tricky knots, which wood bent best, had the best ply, and was the best firewood.

In Ambler's Grove, not five miles from a variety of a healthy stand of foothill trees, Beauvais knew that the aspen and poplar and birch and cottonwood provided leaf food for deer, elk, and buffalo and the tall sight of them pointed native people to streams, which meant sources for water and game fish, animals, shade, and lodge poles. His talents took him to heat and bend and cure iron to many uses, make wagon wheels centered by hubs and bound by iron. Also, he could fish with the best of men in all kinds of waters. It was a revelation too to new friends that the man was adept with a heavy needle on leather. All would agree that Bart Beauvais was born for the west.

And now he knew what signal to watch for in the night, in the foothills of the mountains above Ambler's Grove and the lake that had been built just above and beyond the town by construction of a dam. A dam that might, with implosion, go down river in a night.

Such was it when he came into Ambler's Grove, Colorado, August 7, 1872, not five miles from a variety of a healthy stand of foothill trees. He was 27 years old, unmarried, wore blond locks in a free-fall on the back of his neck, exerted energy sitting at a saloon table or leaning at the bar where his eyes, just as on the trail, never sat still on one subject but made use of their sly and circumspect mobility.

Nobody knew he was a dead shot with a rifle and pistol. Up under his seat on the wagon drawn by his oxen pair, Beauvais carried a Winchester 1873 Carbine Caliber. He'd won it on a bet with his oxen team. On his belt he carried a Colt, rarely out of the holster. He thought he might remember the last time he pulled it free, but it would have been with honor and would take some time to bring back the first circumstance.

And it was Skinned who gathered a new bit of news, slipped close to Beauvais in the saloon, and whispered, "There's a line camp on the far edge of Lyman's G-Bar-4, at the end where the creek withers away onto the prairie. I'd never sleep in a place like that 'cause some of the routers like to use them. Anyways, I was sleepin' in a pile of hay real comfortable when they woke me, and it was the Big German, Louie Blusten, the one with that loud voice who was talking about blowin' up the dam next Tuesday, floodin' out the town, come larrupin' in in the middle of the night when everybody was gone high-tailin' and claimin' the whole place."

"Hell, Skinned, there's only three places in town; the saloon, the store, and the rooming house, which ain't claimin' much."

"He talks like the whole place, the whole town all the way to the creek, would be his once the upper lake runs its way down past it all. That's enough, ain't it, to make somethin' of it?"

Beauvais was thinking already. "When's he planning it, Skinned? Did he say a definite day, time?"

"Come Tuesday night, after midnight sometime, they'll blow the dam up. I heard him say they'd be at the line camp and be out of sight for a whole day, so that means Monday they leave town some time and go into hidin'."

"Time enough for us to get some things done. If we try to

132

stop them at the dam, some will be killed. So we do up a surprise for them."

He leaned over to Skinned and said six names. "Tell them on the sly to meet me here with their wagons and teams on Monday, east of town. Tell 'em to load up with rolling logs, half dozen 30-foot beams, and lots of planks, lots of 'em."

The force gathered as instructed, all the supplies on hand, the men ready, the wagons ready.

The saloon was the first to be moved, after it was jacked up, beamed and aimed for the planks lined with roller logs. The new target resting place was less than 100 yards away, but up a slight incline. All the loose equipment inside the saloon was pulled out and placed on the now-empty wagons and all the wagons gone ahead to be emptied for multi-trips. The same would be done for the other two buildings.

In three and a half hours, with the oxen Reynard and Briscoe exerting much of the initial pull, helped by a good dozen mules, the Lake Paradise Saloon was settled on a new surface and Ambler's Grove was newly constituted in the territory, thieves be damned. The store and the rooming house, already emptied of much loose property, followed in succession, with exultation and hilarity filling the air with each success.

Men worked doggedly to reload each building and utilize every wagon as soon as it was unloaded, with Bart Beauvais constantly on the prod to get men to work harder, faster, to stay ahead of the bandits who wanted to steal a town ... and to soon send a message to a blonde about in the foothills.

Even in his haste to get things done, Beauvais made notes on the qualities of the roller logs, the long beams, the travel planks on which the three enormous loads were moved in the night. His education was still on-going.

Before the dawn flash on Tuesday, the move done, the buildings in their new places, Ambler's Grove was fully re-constituted, certified, enforced with new law, the bomb or bombs went off at the dam site, and hundreds of tons of water rushed out over what had been Ambler's Grove, hiding all the original signs of the Lake Paradise Saloon, the rooming house, and the general store.

When Louie Blusten and his gang rode into town, expecting to claim the ruins of what might have Ambler's Grove, they were surprised to see the new lake sitting where the town used to be … and higher on a lift of land, sitting in the sun, and sitting on dry ground, the Paradise Lake Saloon, the A/G General Store and Hillary's Rooming House, all of course were surrounded by a small army of deputies lead by the newly sworn-in sheriff, Bart Beauvais.

When Blusten's hat was ripped off his head by one carefully-aimed shot, he and his gang turned tail and were never seen again.

It was on the very night, up in the foothills, a series of lights occasionally was shone into the darkness by Kurgeth Kate, and answered, in distinct anticipation, by Bart Beauvais whose oxen were temporarily housed in a lean-to that was to become the livery in Ambler's Grove.

About the Author

Thomas F. Sheehan served in the 31st Infantry, Korea, 1951-52, and graduated Boston College, 1956. Books include *Epic Cures; Brief Cases, Short Spans; The Saugus Book; This Rare Earth & Other Flights; Ah, Devon Unbowed; Reflections from Vinegar Hill.* eBooks include *Korean Echoes (nominated for a Distinguished Military Award)*, *The Westering,* (nominated for National Book Award); from *Danse Macabre* are *Murder at the Forum, Death of a Lottery Foe, Death by Punishment, An Accountable Death and Vigilantes East. A Collection of Friends, From the Quickening, In the Garden of Long Shadows, The Nations, Where Skies Grow Wide, Cross Trails, The Cowboys, Between Mountain and River, Beside the Broken Trail,* and *Catch a Wagon to the Stars* were published by Pocol Press, and *Six Guns, Inc.,* by *Nazar Look,* in Romania. Sheehan has multiple works at these sites: *Rosebud, Linnet's Wings, Serving House Journal, Copperfield Review, KYSO Flash, La Joie Magazine, Soundings East, Literary Orphans, Indiana Voices Journal, Frontier Tales, Western Online Magazine, Provo Canyon Review, Nazar Look, Eastlit, Rope & Wire Magazine, Ocean Magazine, The Literary Yard, Green Silk Journal, Fiction on the Web, The Path, Faith-Hope and Fiction, The Cenacle, etc.* Sheehan's tales have produced 30 Pushcart nominations, and five Best of the Net nominations (and one winner) and short story awards from *Nazar Look* for 2012-2015. *Swan River Daisy* was recently released by KY Stories and *Back Home in Saugus*, 200 pages, 90,000 words, and a chapbook, *Small Victories for the Soul*, are on proposal. (His Amazon Author's Page, Tom Sheehan – is on the Amazon site.)

www.ingramcontent.com/pod-product-compliance
Lightning Source LLC
Chambersburg PA
CBHW011031260626
47153CB00019B/2915